THE UNWANTED

The gift that gives

PETER TONNA

ISBN: 978-0-6450264-3-6 (e-book)
ISBN: 978-0-6450264-7-4 (Paperback)

poetebooks@gmail.com
www.poete.com.au/books

Contents

Prologue

What is a gift worth? Does it depend on the gift itself or on what the gift means to the person receiving it? I've discovered that the greatest gifts are not the most valuable; rather, they are the priceless ones. They may be given once but they are received throughout a lifetime. There comes a point in your life when you realize that what you want and what you need are entirely different things. You can become so distracted chasing what you want that you miss the very thing you need the most. The gift waits to be received with not only open hands but also an open heart.

Seven Years Earlier

*In this world you will have trouble. But take heart!
I have overcome the world*

– John 16:33 (NIV)

Helen Davis

Helen grabs her handbag and whips it over her shoulder. Her colleague agreed to start her evening shift at the orphanage earlier than usual because Helen needs the extra time to prepare for a special evening.

"See you tomorrow," Helen says as she dashes out the door.

"Have a great night," replies her colleague.

She waits at a red traffic light, drumming her fingers on the steering wheel while bopping and humming along to a familiar tune on her favorite radio station, Hits of Yesteryear. The neon lights of a bottle shop sign in the distance catch her eye. A thought pops into her head—a fine bottle of red would be a nice accompaniment to the special celebration meal she has planned. Her husband does enjoy an alcoholic beverage with dinner every now and then. She assents to the thought and pulls into the bottle shop parking lot.

She wanders the aisles and inspects the bottles with elaborate labels. Not familiar with any of the brands, she reasons that the fancier the label, the better the wine. She's by no means a wine connoisseur; she hardly drinks. A watered-down shandy at Christmas is her standard yearly intake. She finally settles on a mid-range bottle of French Cabernet Sauvignon called "Chateau Saint-Emilion." The attendant greets her and grabs the bottle, looks at the label, and nods with approval.

"That's a nice drop. Special occasion?"

"Yes." She beams with enthusiasm. "It's my tenth wedding anniversary today. I'm preparing a surprise meal for my husband."

"Congratulations," he says, finalizing the transaction. "Have a great night."

Helen appreciates the well wishes and thanks him as she leaves.

∞

Helen's husband bursts through the front door of their home. He hurries to the bedroom, grabs a large suitcase from the closet and throws it on the bed. Frantically, he

8

clears out his closet and cabinet, shoving his clothes into the suitcase with no neat order. He rushes to the bathroom vanity, picks out his razors, shaver and toothbrush, and tosses them on top of the clothes. He zips it up and sprints out the bedroom, bulging suitcase in hand. On his way out, he pauses by the kitchen counter to pull an envelope from his back pants pocket. He places it on the kitchen counter, then runs out the front door. The hum of a parked, running car awaits him. A young blond lady sits in the driver's seat. He throws the suitcase in the back seat and jumps into the front passenger seat. She drives off into the darkening evening.

∞

Helen bumps the front door open with her shoulder. "Honey … honey, I'm home."
She tucks the Cabinet Sauvignon under her arm as she wrestles to retrieve her key from the lock. "Hope you're hungry. I'm making something special tonight." She wins the battle and retrieves her key, adding, "we really need to get this lock fixed." She closes the door behind her and remains still, waiting for a response or a sound to confirm his presence. But there's complete silence. Concerned, she calls out again. "Honey?" Helen remains quiet, but there's still no response. She places her handbag and

bottle on the kitchen counter, unaware of the envelope sitting there, and makes the rounds to every room in the house. She mumbles to herself, "he should be home by now." Her thoughts meander, quickly thinking the worst. Maybe he's had an accident? It's unlike like him not to send her a message if he's going to be late. After a thorough search of the whole house, there's no sign of him. She returns to the kitchen to retrieve her phone from her handbag. She's about to call him when she notices the envelope on the counter. At first glance, she assumes it's a regular piece of mail … but there's something different about this envelope. Then, she notices that the only thing on the front of the envelope is her name, written by her husband's hand. She's gripped by a feeling of unease. The muscles in her throat tighten and she gulps unconsciously. The moment triggers a repressed memory from her childhood; the heart-wrenching moment her father walked out on her and her mother, never to be heard from again. She was devastated to feel that her father didn't love her and held a subconscious belief that she was to blame for his departure. She tries to ignore her initial feeling and entertains the brief notion that it's a romantic note from her husband. That he wants to meet her at L'Amour, the fanciest restaurant in town, to celebrate their anniversary. But she knows that would be out-of-character for her husband. He's not the romantic type, never has been, so why would he start now? The longer she mulls over the envelope's contents, the more anxiety takes hold of her. Trembling, she puts down the phone and breathes in deeply. Dismissing the possibility of a rare romantic act, she succumbs to the most likely reality that the contents indicate an outcome more bad than good. Her thoughts turn to her marriage; she tries to recall any signs of problems. Nothing serious comes to mind apart from a few customary spousal squabbles endured by all couples. Nor could she recall any hint of discontentment from him.

Bewildered, Helen stares at the envelope. Her anxiety increases with every passing moment. She tries to remain calm, but her breathing increases in intensity, a slight quiver escorting each exhale. Tentatively, she reaches for the envelope and slides it closer. She pulls out the letter like she's disarming an explosive device. Her fearful eyes follow the words on the page. Then, a flutter, and an unrestrained flood of emotion submerges her vision. The overwhelming surge forms streams of grief down her cheeks. Her deep breaths turn into gasps. Each word she reads is a sledgehammer to her heart. Disoriented, she instinctively places her hand on her chest to stop her already broken heart from falling out of her chest. She sobs aloud, throws the letter to the ground and moves toward the bedroom, not yet believing that what she read is really happening. Sapped of strength, she leans on the walls to keep herself from falling down. She stumbles into the bedroom and opens the closet. In stunned silence, she stands there, her gasps for air momentarily ceased. The left side of the closet, where her husband's clothes once hung, is now bare. Unutilized clothes hangers are all that remain. To Helen, this confirms the contents of the letter. The reality of abandonment knocks her to the ground—she drops like a bag of bricks. Anguish grips her as she weeps uncontrollably.

"No … no … no!"

Amanda Grace

Amanda stares out her bedroom window, gazing up at the stars. Perched on her bed, surrounded by the late-night darkness, legs folded, she tightly embraces a pillow like it's her closest companion. She looks down at her phone placed squarely in front of her, before picking it up. The movement triggers the screen to glow, illuminating the indecision on her face. She swipes and dials, watches the phone dialing; when the call connects, she places it to her ear.

"Hey," she says softly. "Can we catch up before class tomorrow? I need to see you." She listens. "Yeah … yeah, I'm okay. Um … I'm tired, gonna go to bed. I'll see you then … Love you … bye." She puts the phone down and moves aside the pillow she's been clutching. She places her hands on her lower abdomen, caressing it gently.

∞

Amanda leans against the fence outside the school gates, focused intently on a lone dandelion flower reaching for life through a small crack in the concrete surrounds. Her boyfriend Dylan approaches.

"Hey babe." He draws closer to kiss her forehead. Concerned by her lack of response, he asks, "Mandy, you okay?"

"I, uh … I'm," she says. She looks him straight in the eyes. "I'm pregnant." He steps back. Unconsciously, his hands rise to his forehead, sweeping through his hair in disbelief. He turns his back toward her with his hands clasped behind his neck, staring at the ground. Amanda grows agitated in the face of his disengagement.

"Well?" She raises her voice.

He turns around. His wandering eyes suggest he's thinking of the right words to say.

"What are you going to do?"

"What am *I* going to do?" She says, frustrated. "How about what are *we* going to do?"

"Yeah … yeah, that's what I meant," he says unconvincingly.

The school bell rings in the background, signaling the start of first period.

"We need to talk about this at lunch," she says.

"Yeah … sure."

Amanda leans toward him, anticipating an embrace, but he doesn't acknowledge her. He walks away swiftly. She's surprised. It's unlike him to leave her without some expression of parting affection … but she excuses his negligence with the sudden shock of her announcement.

∞

As she waits for Dylan at their usual lunchtime hangout spot, Amanda grows increasingly anxious. She tries to pacify her anxiety by shaking her legs intensely and nibbling her fingernails. She keeps scanning the playground until she can't take it any longer. With seven minutes to spare before the bell signals the end of lunch break, she hastily gets up to search for him. Finally, she spots him in the distance with his usual circle of friends, laughing and mucking around. She rushes toward him but stops shy of the group, not wanting to be surrounded by the unruly herd. She starts trying to get his attention.

"Dyl," she calls. He doesn't acknowledge her, lost in the jovial crowd. She calls louder. "Dylan!" This gets his attention. He stares blankly at her while his mates continue to banter among themselves. Amanda stares back at him, eyes wide open; she motions with her hands, suggesting, *aren't you forgetting something?* For a brief moment, they stare at each other.

"We were meant to meet up, remember?" She says as she places her hands on her hips. The bell rings.

"I forgot."

"Well, can we catch up after school?"

"Sure," he says, shrugging his shoulders. She shakes her head as he walks off with his mates.

∞

Amanda ponders the fate of the lone dandelion. It's been stepped on and lies helpless, crushed on the concrete, its once-vibrant yellow radiance now dulled and in pieces. She checks the time again. 4:11 pm, and there's still no sign of Dylan. She attempts to call him for the fourth time. When she gets his voicemail, she lets out an exasperated grunt and hangs up. She figures there's no point in leaving another message, finally resigned to the likelihood he's not going to show up. Satisfied she's waited long enough, she hangs her head and goes home.

The day's events replay through Amanda's mind, keeping her awake. She sits up, grabs her phone, and swipes through photos of herself and Dylan. What once made her smile, she now views with indifference. She's unsure what to make of his reaction but still clings to the hope that maybe he just needs a little time to get used to the new reality. She reasons that his response is a natural reaction for any teenage boy in his situation. To give him the space she thinks he needs, she decides not to reach out to him for a few days.

∞

Amanda paces the school grounds solemnly during her lunch break, in her own world, unfazed by the energetic exuberance of the other students surrounding her. She stops in her tracks as she spots Dylan in the distance beneath the hundred-year-old willow that's been there since the school was built. He's talking to someone leaning against the trunk. She can't quite make out who it is; the hanging foliage obstructs her view. She maintains her distance and maneuvers into a position where she can see who Dylan is talking with. He lifts his hand, like he's caressing someone's face. Amanda hastens to a better vantage point. Each step reveals a little more of this mystery person as Dylan leans in for a kiss. In that instant, the air is sucked from her. He's with another girl. He pulls back from the kiss and looks out across the playground. His eyes meet Amanda's in the distance. He seems unperturbed that she caught him kissing another girl. He takes the girl's hand and leads her behind the willow trunk, hiding them both from Amanda's view. Her mouth falls open in disbelief, and she stands there motionless. The only movement is the silent heartbreak spilling down her face. She's devastated, not so much by the kiss, but by his blatant disregard, as if she meant nothing to him. Snapping out of her dazed stupor, she wraps both arms around her chest to hold herself together. She scurries away to a secluded corner of the playground to get away from everyone. Leaning against a wall, she slides down to the ground, then embraces herself in the fetal position. She's realized the reality of the situation. Dylan wants nothing to do with her and the pregnancy. She's in this alone.

∞

Amanda spent a week moving on from Dylan, deleting, removing and throwing out any reminders of him and their time together. A type of catharsis she hoped would make her feel better, and it did for a short time. Yet one remnant of their past remains. There are only two people in the world that know her secret, and the other wants nothing to do with it. She has mixed feelings and continues to agonize over which step to take next. Since her childhood, prominent messages in the media and prevailing public opinion have been quite clear—there is only one option for someone in her situation: seventeen, on the cusp of college, and with her whole life ahead of her. Yet, deep down, she suspects that the loudest voice isn't necessarily the right voice. Buried beneath the stressful thought of becoming a single teenage mother, a persistent sense of unease gently taps against her conscious like a faint heartbeat yearning for attention. Finally, she surrenders to the weight of her fear … at the expense of what her conscious whispers is not the right thing to do.

Amanda lies wide awake. Intensely, she ponders the choice she thinks she's settled on. Staring at her phone, she waits for 11:59 pm to tick over to midnight. She lifts her head a little and peers past her bedroom door. The coast seems clear. She peels off the covers and sits on the edge of her bed. Already dressed in her hoodie and jeans, she slips on her shoes and quietly makes her way downstairs. A loose nail squeaks, and she winces, coming to a swift standstill. She remains still for a moment to ensure the sudden noise doesn't wake her parents. After a few moments of reassuring silence, she continues toward the front door as quietly as possible. She fumbles for the car keys in her jean pocket and carefully opens the car parked in the driveway, pressing her tongue against her upper lip, making as little noise as possible.

Repeatedly, she looks up at her parent's bedroom window for any sign of them waking. She unlocks the handbrake and backs the car on to the street. Satisfied the car is a good distance from her home, she hops in, starts the transmission and drives away from her home. It's a relatively short journey, yet it feels like the longest ride of her life, the rhythmic lull of tires on asphalt and the sound of her own thoughts her only companions.

Finally, Amanda pulls into the parking lot of a 24/7 medical clinic. She'd decided to avoid a clinic in her own town so as not to bump into anyone she might know. She opens the entrance door just wide enough to slide in sideways, a part of her hoping she won't be noticed. Apart from the receptionist, she's the only one there. She smiles at Amanda standing despondently near the entry with her arms folded and head lowered.

"How can I help you dear?" Amanda makes her way to the counter shyly and speaks softly.

"Um … I'm here for…" Not wanting to say the word "abortion" aloud, she grabs a brochure from the counter and shows the receptionist.

"Ah, say no more, my dear. Take a seat and the doctor will be with you soon." As Amanda walks to the nearest seat, the receptionist adds, "don't worry, dear, it's just a simple procedure." Amanda takes a seat and waits miserably to be summoned. In her mind, she replays the words spoken so casually by the receptionist, *it's just a simple procedure*. She believes that it is, physically, a simple procedure. But she thinks to herself, *it's more than a physical procedure, isn't it? Surely, there are psychological and emotional aspects to it ... otherwise why can't I find peace with this decision?* She scans the brochure for any mention of such effects, but finds nothing.

Her deep thought is interrupted by the high-pitched squeak of the door she's waiting to enter. The doctor fixes her gaze on Amanda and motions with her head to come on in. She puts down the brochure, her eyes beginning to well. She pauses for a moment, overwhelmed by a stark feeling that she's entering a place of no return. Again, she convinces herself that this is the most common way of handling the issue—this is what's best for her. Both of her hands grip the corners of the seat, and she thrusts herself up. She slowly makes her way toward the surgery room, placing both hands on her lower abdomen as if to say "sorry" and "goodbye."

Amanda has a dreadful sense she's about to destroy the "mother" inside her. Despite bodily having risen, she looks back at the seat, feeling as though her soul remains there on that seat, watching her walk away. She fades into the surgery room, and the door closes behind her.

Doctor Thomas Fletcher

The congregation begins to spill out of the church while the organist plays the last few bars of "Joy to the World" to conclude the Christmas Eve evening mass. Thomas and his wife Sophie leave the service, cheerfully hand-in-hand, their young daughter Ruby between them. Well wishes, "Merry Christmas" and "have a great day," are exchanged as they maneuver through the excited crowd huddled on the church forecourt. They reach the steps that descend to the parking lot, and Thomas looks down at Ruby with a cheeky grin.

"Are you ready?" Ruby nods with excitement. Thomas and Sophie lift Ruby above the stairs. In unison, a joyful "wheeee" accompanies their descent. Ruby laughs all the way down. When they reach the bottom of the stairs, Ruby blurts out "gen!" In toddler-speak, she means "again."

"Oh, sweetheart, it's already dark and you need to get your sleep. You want to get up early to open all your presents, don't you?" Sophie says. Ruby nods in agreement. They reach their car; Thomas heads for the driver's seat while Sophie takes Ruby to the passenger-side back seat to strap her in. Before Sophie can strap her in, Ruby jumps out of the infant car seat and lunges toward Thomas from behind, poking her head between the two front seats.

"Daddy, can open prezzen tonight?" She asks. Thomas looks past her to Sophie, not quite sure how to handle the situation. Sophie holds up her index finger and quietly mouths, "one."

He looks back at Ruby, "Ok, sweetie," he says. "But just one present, and the rest in the morning, okay?"

"Okay, daddy." Ruby kisses him on the forehead. "Love you, daddy."

"Love you too, precious."

Thomas comes to a red light as joyful singing fills the car. *Good tidings we bring to you and your kin, we wish you a Merry Christmas and a Hap-py ... New ... Year.* Cheers and laughter follow the crescendo. The light turns green, and Thomas proceeds into the intersection. His gaze shifts to Sophie, still laughing from the joyful singing. He adores the way she laughs. Briefly, they stare at each other in admiration. Lost in the moment, Thomas momentarily becomes unaware of his surrounds. At first, he doesn't notice the sudden appearance of headlights in his peripheral view from outside Sophie's passenger window. In a split second, those headlights glare a mere inch from her window.

A sickening smack, and the passenger side of the car crumples like aluminum foil. After rising slightly in the air, then tipping sideways in slow motion, their car wobbles on its side. The previously silent night is disrupted by the incessant howl of the car horn and the hissing of a gasket.

∞

A slight drizzle accompanies the chill in the air, so it's bitingly cold. The weather reflects uncomfortably how Thomas is feeling. He limps despondently into Burkwood Cemetery. One arm in a sling, the other tightly clutching two white roses. He flinches with every step, but the physical pain pales in comparison to that weighing on his heart. He stops in front of two headstones, one bigger than the other. Staring at them in silence, he is overcome by despair. His body crumples limply under the profound weight tugging on his heart, and he falls to his knees. Thomas places a rose on each headstone and caresses the names engraved in the marble. He weeps uncontrollably, before rubbing his face in sudden frustration.

He looks up at the sky and begs angrily, "why?" He aches to understand why this has happened, although he is aware that no answer could possibly placate his grief. In the ensuing silence, while he searches the heavens, his breathing intensifies. Gasping deeply, each breath increasing in anger, he raises his clenched fist at the sky. Through gritted teeth, he wails. "Why!?"

The pigeons, which had been perched comfortably in the nearby elm, retreat noisily.

Max Harris

Max rubs his eyes, weary from his daily afternoon nap. He slides out of bed and makes his way to the kitchen to check the refrigerator for something to eat. There's only half a bottle of sludgy yellow-tinged milk and a slice of furred green pizza. Accustomed to rarely finding anything edible to appease his hunger, he slumps into the lounge room and turns on the television. He flicks through the channels until he finds his favorite cartoon, "Special Troop Force," a very popular choice among five- or six-year-old boys. The first episode of a six-episode, three-hour marathon. He watches and waits till his parents come home, hoping they'll bring him something to eat.

Max is absorbed by the final episode of the marathon; it's his favorite part where the Force is about to triumph over the dark armies of evil once and for all. His attention is interrupted by the startling slam of the front door. Mumbles and footsteps become louder down the hallway, accompanied by the dulled clinking of glass bottles wrapped in brown paper bags. His young ears are well acquainted with the distinctive sound. His gaze locks on them with trepidation as they walk past. His father sees him first.

"What are you looking at, good for nothing?" His mother laughs out loud.

"Useless boy," she adds.

Although Max has heard disparaging remarks like these many times before, he is deflated every time.

"Go to your room and stay there," his father shouts from the distance, as they move toward the kitchen.

Max quietly provides the voice for his Captain Figo figurine, the main character of "Special Troop Force." Like every other night, the battle between good and evil plays out on Max's bed under the dim glow of a table lamp. The enemies alternate between his dinosaur figurines and a few empty cans of soft drink on which he's drawn eyes and sharp teeth. Sometimes both evil forces combine in an ultimate showdown for the universe. No matter the nemesis, though, Captain Figo always wins. Max tires himself play acting, and his heavy head falls slowly toward the pillow. He props himself back up again; he needs to use the bathroom. He knows to stay out of sight when his parents have their nightly feasts—he doesn't want to trigger their unbridled verbal abuse. He peeks through the slightly open door, waiting till the coast is clear. He scurries to the bathroom. Within moments, he returns and swiftly closes the door behind him; however, he leaves it slightly ajar, peeking out to ensure he wasn't seen. This time, they didn't see him; he breathes a sigh of relief and closes the door. He doesn't bother to ask for a little something from their nightly smorgasbord. Ever since he could remember, none of his parents' feast treats would soothe a child's hunger pains. The usual assortment sits on the kitchen table. A range of clear and amber liquids. White, pink, or pale blue candies the size of a fingernail. These are usually consumed under a lingering smoke haze.

Tonight, there is a special dessert—a fine white powder to finish their feast.

∞

Somewhat surprisingly, Max wakes to complete silence. Until now, his sleep had been interrupted, his parents' rowdy feast repeatedly jolting him awake throughout the night. His sleepy eyes peer toward the window, trying to ascertain the time. The first shards of dawn's sunlight begin to pierce the curtains. He gets out of bed, opens the door a little and surveys the scene before venturing out. His parents are at the kitchen table, motionless apart from the occasional sudden twitch or subtle moan. Hesitantly, he approaches them. He stands near them in hope of some reaction, but they don't acknowledge him. Eventually, he speaks up.

"I'm hungry."

His father, slumped on the table, lifts his brows slowly in reaction to his voice. He struggles to open his eyes but speaks groggily. "Can't you do anything for yourself? Go away."

His mother, leaning back in her chair, leans forward and chimes in.

"You're a mistake." She points her finger at him unsteadily. "I wish you were never born." She slumps back again in her chair.

He flinches at the words. She hadn't ever said that before. Hearing those words for the first time drains the life from his eyes as her vicious declaration rips out his last remaining ounce of self-worth. In that moment, he truly believes his mother. *He is a mistake.* His father leans forward, grabs him by the shirt, and throws him to the ground. The throw lacks thrust, but Max drops to the floor, utterly weakened by his mother's remark. They burst into mocking laughter. Immediately, like water breaking through a dam, tears flood his face. He is hurt not by the fall but by the wrecking ball of their ridicule. He runs to his room and throws himself onto his bed, face on his pillow.

∞

Abruptly, Max lifts his face from his pillow. Incredibly, he had drifted off to sleep. The uneasy night and life-sapping torment had wearied him to the point of exhaustion. He sits up on his bed and remains still for a moment, listening intently for any kind of sound. The afternoon is wholly silent apart from a car parking in the street outside. He gets out of bed and makes his way cautiously into the kitchen. His parents are still at the table. His mother leans back in her chair, head slumped back and arms flopped open on either side. His father's torso rests on the table with one arm outstretched, the other hanging downward. Max stares at them, unfazed, until he's startled by a knock at the front door. He goes to see who it is, partially opens the door, and peeks upward. It's Mr. Balouch, the owner of the property, who pops over every Friday afternoon to collect the rent. Mr. Balouch expected to be greeted at face height; on seeing no one, his face crumples in confusion. Looking down, he spots Max.

"Ah," he says, surprised. "Hello, young man. I'm here to collect the rent." As he talks, Max slowly opens the door wider. "Could you please get your mommy or dah …" Mr. Balouch trails off mid-sentence as he sees

Max's parents in the background, passed out at the kitchen table. "Oh my!"

∞

Max watches the commotion from the back of a police car as police and paramedics swarm the property. He munches gratefully on a sandwich given to him by a police officer, still clutching his Captain Figo figurine. It's been a good while since he ate anything that wasn't stale or out of date. Intently, he observes Mr. Balouch being interviewed by a police officer. He's glad he came when he did—in a way, the landlord rescued him. The more he thinks about it, the happier he becomes, his little legs swinging in contentment. His joy turns to indifference at the sight of his mother being wheeled out on a stretcher, barely conscious and mumbling incoherently. His father follows, unconscious, with a breathing mask and bags of fluid connected to his arms. Both are bundled into an ambulance and driven away, sirens blaring.

Bruce Douglas

Bruce shuffles through the latest bunch of bills, each with an ominous warning stamped in red ink. He seems to receive them faster than he can pay them. His pension, coupled with his wife's income from working at the library, was just enough to get them through life. Since her passing, though, living has been a struggle in more ways than one. He would work if he could, but the injuries he sustained in combat mean he can't endure twenty minutes of labor without his arms and legs succumbing to shooting pain. He pushes the bills to one side of the kitchen table, sighing concernedly and running his hand through his silver hair. On the other side of the kitchen table sits a mahogany display case the size of a shoebox. He gazes at it for a moment, before hesitantly pulling the box toward him. He opens it. A box this size could hold an array of treasure and trinkets, yet this one holds only two lonely items. He picks up his late wife's gold wedding ring and caresses it with his thumbs. He places the ring in his shirt pocket and focuses on the other item. Right in the center of the display case, in pride of place, lays the symbol of his bravery. A Purple Heart medal, awarded to him for coming within inches of losing his life on the battlefields of the Vietnam War. Along with his wife's wedding band, it's his most cherished possession. Faded imprints mark the green felt on either side of the medal—other medals once accompanied his Purple Heart. To Bruce, it represents the near-sacrifice of his life for everything he believed in. But as much as he cherishes this last medal, he can't bear to part with his wife's wedding ring. Not because of the monetary value, but because of what it means—it's a part of her that will always be with him. Since he recently parted with his own wedding band, it's one of the only tangible symbols of their fifty-one years together. He gets up from the table, tucks the mahogany case under his arm, and walks out the door. On his way, he thoroughly considers all possible options, hoping he can avoid surrendering his treasured medal. What is normally a twelve-minute hobble into the town center takes him over twenty minutes. By the time he reaches the pawnshop, he concedes that there's no other option. He enters the store he's already visited several times before. Standing still near the entrance, he pulls the mahogany case from under his arm. He stares at the box in his hands, in deep deliberation, until the shop attendant interrupts him.

"Mr. Douglas, how can I help you today?"

Bruce walks up to the counter, wooden box in hand, and places it on the counter.

∞

Dejected, Bruce sits at his kitchen table. Head lowered, he gazes at the empty mahogany display case in front of him. The faded imprints of seven medals are all that remain. He retrieves his wife's wedding ring from his shirt pocket and places it in the center of the box where his Purple Heart once lay. He closes the box, and his attention shifts to the results of his latest trade—one hundred and ninety-five dollars. To Bruce, the cash doesn't represent the cost of the medal itself; it represents the value of his very life. A sense of unease begins to well within, and he glares at the money with disdain. The same thought repeats in his mind. *I risked my life for one hundred and ninety-five dollars ... I almost lost my life for one hundred and ninety-five dollars.* The more he entertains the thought, the more agitated he becomes. The feelings of insignificance, coupled with the reality of his loneliness, weigh heavy on his mind. A tremor overtakes him, his age-lined face wrinkling further; he places his hand on his chin to calm the shudder. For the first time in his life, this battle-hardened and robust soldier, who has let no one and nothing deter his resolve, has succumbed to defeat, surrendering to his perceived insignificance and abandonment. Unappreciated and abandoned by his country—the very country he fought and risked his life for—which has now left him to fend for himself. Abandoned by his closest war buddies, all of whom have since passed on. And, although he does not blame her, abandoned by his wife.

∞

Bruce washes his teacup while looking out the kitchen window at the pouring rain. A knock at the front door breaks his gaze. He hobbles to the door, but no one's there. He sees a small truck parked out front, emblazoned with "Repo." Bruce continues to watch, not quite sure what's happening, as several men scramble in the heavy rain. Men hustle up the pathway into his home; Bruce stands aside as they enter with caps on, looking downward, avoiding eye contact. He attempts to speak to them as they file past one by one, but they rush by quicker than Bruce can form words. The last repo man in the line approaches Bruce with clipboard in hand, a "manager" patch emblazoned across his chest.

"Bruce Douglas?" Bruce nods. "We're here to possess payment for outstanding bills."

Bruce is bewildered. "I thought I had more time …"

"Sorry, sir … we have our orders."

Bruce acquiesces; he's all but given up the fight in life. He watches as they carry out items one by one: antique chairs, tables and cabinets that have lasted through fifty years of marriage. Rhythmic thuds and thumps sound throughout his home. The clunks of earthenware and the clatter of cutlery resonate from the kitchen. The manager jots down the items being taken to the truck while Bruce stands miserably in the middle of the lounge room. The raid progressively quiets down as the men leave one by one. The only other remaining repo man approaches the manager with one last item in hand. It's the mahogany case, open to show him the ring.

"No!" Bruce says urgently. "That's my wife's wedding ring." He reaches out his hand in desperation. "Please don't take it."

Both men look at him but remain silent. The manager motions with his head, to the man holding the case, to take it to the truck. Bruce is deflated; his pleading arm drops with a quiver of the lip as he watches the treasured possession being taken away.

"Wait." The manager stops the man before he is out the door. Bruce lifts his head, daring to assume the manager has had a change of heart. The manager has noticed a lone ornate antique frame on the fireplace mantle; he grabs it to give to the man before he walks out. It contains a photograph from Bruce's wedding day.

"Please … let me keep something of my wife," Bruce begs. The manager is unmoved by his request. He speaks again. "At least, let me keep the photograph." The manager nods and removes the photograph from the frame, passing it to Bruce before handing the frame to the repo man. He tightly holds the photograph against his chest. Bruce and the manager are all that remain in the echoing and empty lounge room.

"Sir. I've been advised to let you know that you are required to vacate the premises by 4.00 pm," he says while scribbling on his clipboard. "Do you have someone you can stay with?" He asks this with an air more of formality than concern.

"I have no one."

The manager looks up, as if he had expected him to say that he had some place to go.

"Oh … I'm sure there's a place in town that could take you in." He points over his shoulder with his pen in the direction of town.

"All the best, sir." He nods, then walks out, closing the door behind him. Bruce scans his barren surroundings, sighing with deep resignation. His physical existence now resembles how he feels on the inside—empty. He stands motionless, still embracing the photograph, the only thing of value he has left.

Emmanuel

The neighborhood exudes a particular enchantment at this time of year. The flashing rhythmic lights, reflective tinsel, and glowing Santa displays illuminate the peaceful night. Unit 37 patrols the streets. The officers on duty enjoy the shift; hardly any trouble surfaces. They're admiring and commenting on the Christmas yard displays when a call comes in on the radio.

"Unit 37, we have a disturbance in the vicinity of Saint Michael's Church, over." The officer in the passenger seat picks up the radio.

"What seems to be the problem, over?" They listen intently.

"Several residents in the area have reported a child screaming, over." They look at each other with immediate concern.

"Okay, we're onto it, over." The driver speeds up a little.

They pull up out front of the church. They step out and remain still, straining to detect any sound.

"You hear that?"

"Yeah … I think it's coming from over there." They make their way toward the sound; the faint cry gets louder as they approach. Clouds hide the moonlight, making their surroundings pitch-black. Apart from their torches, the only light comes from the nativity scene set up beside the church. This seems to be where the crying is coming from. As they approach the nativity scene, it's evident that the crying is indeed coming from the nativity. Upon reaching the crib, they see a baby crying in distress, wrapped tightly in a blanket, lying in the manger.

"Oh!"

The officer reaches quickly for her radio. "Unit 37 to base, we've got an abandoned baby at Saint Michael's Church … looks like a newborn, over."

"Roger that. Stand by, over."

The other officer tends to the baby, trying to stop him from crying. He notices a note tucked under a fold in the blanket. He plucks it out and unfolds it.

"What is it?"

He gazes at the note with uncertainty. "Looks like a Bible verse …"

"Well … what does it say?"

He looks at her, then back at the note. Before he can read it out, a call comes back over the radio.

"Calling Unit 37. An ambulance is on the way. A child protective services representative will be at the hospital, over."

"Copy that, over." Just as she ends radio communication, an ambulance pulls up behind the police car. She heads toward the ambulance while the other officer stays with the baby.

∞

The doctor finalizes his notes while tending to the baby. Several tests have been conducted to gauge the health of the child. The doctor enters the waiting area to speak to the child protective services representative. There's only one person in the room.

"I assume you're from CPS?"

"Yes." She bounces to her feet and heads toward the doctor. "How is the baby?

They walk to the room where the baby rests.

"I'm afraid it's not good news."

The woman sighs, disappointed.

"We've discovered a congenital heart condition. Unfortunately, it's incurable, so we can only manage it the best we can. I've organized regular ongoing appointments, starting next month, to monitor his progress. We're still waiting on a few results to come in. We'll be in touch if we discover anything further."

"Okay … Thank you doctor."

The woman picks up the baby in her arms, and says softly, "hello there, little man." The baby coos back at her.

∞

The night shift caretaker is startled by the sudden noise at the front door. The enduring quiet at the orphanage at this time of night makes any noise seem louder than it is.

The child protective services representative enters, cradling a baby in one arm.

"Who do we have here?" The caretaker asks. She approaches the baby, hands clasped, resting on her chin, smitten by the baby. "Oh, so adorable!" She caresses his head softly. "What's his name?"

The representative ponders this for a moment.

"I don't know … he was found in the manger of the nativity at Saint Michael's Church."

"In the manger!" The caretaker repeats in disbelief. She gently takes the child and cradles him.

"Well … in that case, we'll call him … Emmanuel."

Presence of the Present

This is the day that the Lord has made;
let us rejoice and be glad in it.

– Psalms 118:24 (ESV)

Abby is awakened by the chatter of the other girls who have just woken up. She rubs her tired face, rolls on her tummy, and slides down the side of the bed. After using the bathroom, she heads to the play area. Lost in her own world, she sings a tune, making up words like all toddlers do. Joyfully, she constructs a house with building blocks on the play mat. Max loiters in the play area, a consistent early riser due to memories of the past heckling him throughout the night. He's been at the orphanage ever since his parents were taken to the hospital and is the oldest one there. Other children make their way to the play area to slump down on the couch, watching the morning cartoons while waiting for breakfast. Max walks up to Abby and stops beside her for a moment. He swings his foot forward, knocking down the block-house she's been building, then casually walks away. Abby's joy turns to sadness in an instant, and she begins to cry. The other children look on, unsurprised by Max's action, well aware of his disruptive reputation. Emmanuel, affectionately called "Manny," saw what happened and hurries to her side. He pats her on the back.

"Don't cry, Abby, I'll help you build another one." Her crying dissipates slowly, and she rubs her tear-soaked eyes with her fists. Manny grabs the first block, placing it in front of her; she follows his lead. As they're building, Max walks by again and lightly shoves Manny in the back.

"Loser," he mumbles. Manny ignores him and keeps building with Abby.

Amanda is out on the patio, preparing breakfast for the children, oblivious to what has just happened. She opens the sliding door and pokes her head through.

"Okay kids, breakfast is ready." By this time, all the children are lounging in the play area. She opens the door wider to let the rushing horde of children through to take a seat. "Oh, Manny," she says as she suddenly remembers. "We have an appointment at the hospital in an hour, you good to go?"

"Yes, Miss Grace."

"We'll leave as soon as Ms. Davis gets here after breakfast."

He nods with a mouth full of food. Rosie sits opposite him.

"You going to the hospital again, Manny?" She asks.

"Yeah."

"I hope you get better soon."

"I'll be fine. Do you feel better, Rosie?"

"Yeah. Miss Grace gave me medicine yesterday afternoon and told me to rest. I feel much better today."

"That's good." He smiles.

∞

The children are engaged in their usual morning activities. The older children relax in the play area, watching television, while the toddlers color and draw. The in-between-ers remain outside, playing in the large grassy yard that runs off the patio. Today, "Tag" is the game of choice. Ms. Davis enters the orphanage with her trademark stern countenance, squinted eyes and pursed lips. There's a hushed murmur among the children.

"Ms. Davis is here." They quietly warn one another. They're familiar with her firm regime and don't dare to step out of line while she's in charge. Ms. Davis makes her way to the main desk, places her bag down, and takes a seat. She looks out at the children, making sure all is in order. Amanda walks in from the children's bedrooms, having made their beds, and is startled to see her there.

"Oh … morning, Ms. Davis. Didn't hear you come in. Thank-you for covering while I take Manny to the hospital." Ms. Davis glares at her with irritation.

"Yes, well, hurry back, I have things to do."

"Yes, Ms. Davis, I will."

Amanda grabs her bag and heads out the door. "Come along now, Manny, we've got to go," Amanda says.

He gets up from the play area and heads out with her.

"See you later, Manny," Rosie says.

Abby waves. "Fanks for build house wif me," Abby says with an adorable lisp.

Manny waves back at them as he disappears behind the closing door.

∞

Amanda and Manny wait at a red light. Manny stares out his side window. There's a homeless man digging through garbage cans out front of a café. It's Bruce—he's looking for something to eat. Manny watches him intently as he analyzes the morsels of food, sniffing before tasting to test edibility. The diners having their alfresco breakfast take offense at Bruce's presence, and the café owner rushes out to Bruce with broom in hand.

"Get out of here," he yells, brandishing the broom to keep him at a distance. Bruce scurries off with food in

44

hand; he's not one to hang around where he's not wanted. The light changes to green, and Amanda drives on.

"How are you feeling today, Manny?"

"I'm doing great."

"How are you going, Miss Grace?

She smiles, touched by his concern. "I'm doing okay," she says without conviction. A moment of silence follows.

"Miss Grace?"

She lifts her brow and turns her head slightly while keeping her eyes on the road.

"Why are you sad all the time? I mean … you look sad." She glances at Manny, surprised by his observant question. Amanda remains silent, pondering how to respond to this not-so-average seven-year-old. His empathy, wisdom, and kindness are years beyond any child she has ever encountered. She feels a type of reassuring comfort whenever she is with him. She breaks her silence.

"About seven years ago, I made a mistake that … I still regret to this day. I'm trying to make up for it … but the regret doesn't go away."

Manny thinks for a moment before responding. "Unless you forgive yourself, you can't move on from the past."

"That's easier said than done. I think God might be punishing me."

"Oh no, he wouldn't do that," he says without hesitation. "He knows we're not perfect, that's why he sent Jesus to save us. If you ask him from your heart to forgive you, he will. There are consequences to the choices you make in this life, but you don't have to let them keep you down. Jesus can help you through anything … if you let him." Just as he finishes talking, Amanda pulls into the hospital parking lot. She looks at Manny with wonder, not quite sure how to respond to his enlightened words. He smiles at her.

"We're here," he says.

∞

"Hi, we have an appointment with Doctor Singh," says Amanda to the nurse at the desk.

"Oh, Doctor Singh has been relocated to another hospital in the district." She pauses for a moment to look down at her documents. "And… it looks like Doctor Fletcher will be looking after his patients going forward. I'll let him know you've arrived. Please take a seat."

"Thank you," Amanda says as the nurse goes to alert Doctor Fletcher.

They take a seat in the hallway waiting area. Amanda is deep in thought, considering what Manny said to her in the car. She turns to him.

"Can God really forgive me?" She asks.

"There's nothing he won't forgive if we really mean it."

Amanda is comforted by his response yet she finds it hard to believe that it could truly apply to her.

Once a week, Dimples the Clown makes her rounds at the hospital, entertaining the children with jokes, singing, and sleight of hand, leaving a trail of joy and laughter and brightening the mood and lives of the children there. She makes her way down the hall and approaches Amanda and Manny in her bright apparel and oversized shoes.

"Hey guys, I'm Dimples the Clown, how are you going today?"

"Great! How are you, Miss Dimples?" Manny straightens up, responding with delight. Amanda has a big smile on her face as she watches the excitement unfold.

"Well, I'm fantastic now I've bumped into you," she says matter-of-factly, placing her hands on hips.

"Hey, would you like to do a 'funny pose' photo for our hospital fun board?" She waves a Polaroid camera in hand.

"Sure," they both say.

Amanda and Manny do their best "funny pose" while Dimples takes the photo. They both lean into each other. Amanda opens her eyes and mouth wide open, looking shocked, while Manny sticks out his tongue and makes the peace sign with both hands.

Dimples grabs the photograph and shakes it to reveal the picture.

"Great stuff guys, that's a keeper." She admires the photo, then shows it to them. "I'll be sure to put that one on the fun board. Have a great day now."

"You too," Amanda says. Manny waves as she moves on down the hall with her small entourage.

They watch Dimples interact with the other patients as Doctor Fletcher approaches them, preoccupied by his clipboard.

"Emmanuel?" He says.

Amanda sits up in her seat and nods.

"This way."

He leads them to an examination room. Doctor Fletcher reaches out to shake hands with Manny.

"I'm Doctor Fletcher. I'll be looking after you from now on."

"Nice to meet you, Doc." Manny shakes his hand.

"I'm Amanda Grace." She places her hand on her chest, introducing herself. "I'm one of the caretakers at the orphanage."

Before Doctor Fletcher can respond, a siren sounds in the background. Their attention turns to the commotion in the hall. A nurse pokes her head into the room.

"Doctor, we have an emergency situation." She sounds frantic. "A boy's been stabbed, and Doctor Willis hasn't arrived yet."

He turns to Amanda and Manny.

"Please excuse me, I'll be back as soon as I can." He hurries off with the nurse.

"I hope he's going to be okay," says Amanda under her breath. She leans against the examination table, lowering her head in contemplation.

Manny breaks the silence. "How are you trying to make up for it?"

Amanda looks at him, confused. "What?"

"In the car … on our way here. You said you're trying to make up for the mistake you made." Amanda looks down in deliberation, thinking that she may have revealed a little too much. She ponders her response carefully, knowing there's a limit to what you can tell a child.

"I just want to help children who've been neglected and abandoned."

"What you're doing is a good thing, and it might make you feel better. But it won't take away the pain of what happened. Only God can do that." She concentrates intently on what he's saying. "It's a matter of the heart, you have to allow yourself to be forgiven by yourself, and God."

"I really do care for the children," she says in defense.

"I know … I've felt your motherly heart."

She's startled by his response, afraid that he's discovered the center of her secret pain. She wrestles with her thoughts and emotions before asking, "how … ?" She wants to ask how he knows what to say but stops short of asking the question, not wanting to expose her anguish any further. She reasons that his words are coincidental but can't shake the sense of a deeper connection. Like he intuitively knows her somehow. He's the only person that's come close to knowing the burden she's carried alone all this time.

Doctor Fletcher walks back into the room, looking flustered. He heads straight to the utensil area, oblivious of the intense moment that has just occurred in the room.

"I apologize for the wait," he says. Amanda, a little choked-up by the intense conversation, clears her throat.

"That's okay … we understand. How's the boy?"

"He's in a stable condition. He'll recover," the doctor says as he prepares his stethoscope and blood pressure monitor to examine Manny. "I don't know what's wrong with the world when children are being stabbed." He sighs.

"The world loves God less and less," says Manny. "When that happens, anger and hatred grow." Doctor Fletcher looks at him with some annoyance.

"Well … why doesn't God stop it?"

"God gives everyone a free will, to choose to do bad, or good, to love, or to hurt."

"And what about the terrible things that happen outside of our control?"

"That's the reality of living in a fallen world. Bad things happen to people who don't deserve it. But one day, all pain, suffering and sadness won't exist anymore." Doctor Fletcher listens while examining him. He sighs, then proceeds to measure Manny's blood pressure in silence.

"Do you believe in God, doc?" Manny asks.

The question brings him to a standstill. He looks at Manny like it's the first time someone has asked him that question. After a slight pause, he proceeds to observe Manny's blood pressure, looking down at what he's doing, holding the stethoscope in place.

"I used to."

"Well, he still believes in you."

Again, Doctor Fletcher stops what he's doing and looks at Manny, surprised by his enlightened remarks. Manny smiles. Doctor Fletcher looks at Amanda, as if to say, *who is this kid?!* She smiles and shrugs her shoulders. Doctor Fletcher slides the blood pressure cuff off Manny's arm.

"You sure have a lot of wisdom for a young boy," he says as he puts away the medical equipment. "Okay, Emmanuel, I'll need you to have a chest x-ray before we're done for the day." Doctor Fletcher walks toward the doorway, looking for an available nurse.

"Tiffany," he calls, motioning to her to come over. He turns to Manny.

"Nurse Tiffany will take you to get a chest x-ray."

"Okay," he responds. Tiffany smiles, reaches out her hand for Manny to hold, and leads him out of the room.

He turns to Amanda. "He's pretty insightful for his age."

"He sure is." She chuckles. "He's a special kid, not like any other I've known … that's for sure. He's selfless, and he seems to know the right thing to say at the right time." Doctor Fletcher nods. After a brief pause, Amanda asks, "how is Manny's condition?"

"Looking at the last check-up and what I've seen today so far, the situation looks steady. The x-ray will tell us more. How long have you known him?"

"I started working at the orphanage four years ago. Manny, that's what we call him at the orphanage, has been there all his life, since he was found as a newborn."

"Found?"

"Seven years ago, on Christmas Eve. He was found in a manger of a nativity scene out the front of a church." She pauses for a moment, before continuing pensively. "Only a note, a Bible passage to be exact, was found with him." At first, she didn't notice that Doctor Fletcher's countenance had changed. Now, seeing his sadness, she asks, "Doctor … are you okay?"

"Seven years ago … Christmas Eve," he mumbles faintly, gazing downward. She stares at the man with concern and confusion.

"Seven years ago, on Christmas Eve ... I lost my wife and daughter in a motor accident." Amanda's expression turns sympathetic, and she instinctively places her hand on her heart. "A drunk driver ran a red light and hit the passenger side of our vehicle ... I was driving."

"I'm so sorry ... You don't blame yourself, do you?" He looks away, ignoring her question. There's a brief pause.

"The note found with Manny, what did it say?" Amanda notices that he didn't answer her question. She doesn't want to press the matter.

"It said," she says, pausing for a moment, trying to recall the correct wording. Just then, Tiffany returns with Manny.

"We're all done," she says.

"Yep, tell it to me straight, doc, I can take it." Doctor Fletcher is amused by his candor.

"I'll be in touch in the next day or so."

"Okay, Doc."

"Thank you, Doctor Fletcher," Amanda says as she starts to head out the room with Manny. Doctor Fletcher calls out just before she walks out.

"Oh, Amanda." He pulls a card from his shirt pocket. "If you have any concerns, be sure to call." She takes it.

"I will, thank you, Doctor."

∞

"Do you want anything from the shop before we get back?"

"No, I'm good," Manny says. "He's a nice doctor."

Amanda smiles. "Yeah, he is."

"I think he's sad about something that happened in his life." Amanda glances at him in disbelief, thinking to herself, *how does he know this stuff?*

"Why do you say that?" She's curious to know how he knows without confirming his assumptions.

"You can see it in his eyes, there's a deep sadness." He turns to look at Amanda and continues. "Just like the sadness in your eyes." He looks back out his window. They remain silent for the remainder of the trip back to the orphanage. Amanda ponders the events of the morning and Manny's surprising words of wisdom.

Prisoners of Pain

The Lord is close to the brokenhearted
and saves those who are crushed in spirit.

– Psalms 34:18 (NIV)

Ms. Davis pulls into her driveway and hurries inside to dodge the first light of dawn. She's grown anxious regarding sunlight and prefers to exist in perpetual darkness, a bitter form of comfort to accompany the way she feels. The sunlight has been barred from entering her home—the curtains have not been drawn open since her husband left her. She tosses her bag on the kitchen counter, drops down onto the living room armchair, breathes out a long sigh. The incessant thoughts of rejection, coupled with years of sleep deprivation have turned her into a wearied mess. Her face tells this story; bags of worry and stress lines have added the time to her face created by such a burden.

She begins to doze off. Ms. Davis hasn't slept in her bedroom for the last seven years. This is where the painful memory is most vivid. She's jolted awake by a thought. Constantly, thoughts punctuate and haunt her resting hours. She rubs her face in frustration. She wants to forget but there's a nagging part of her that doesn't want to move on. Not until she receives an explanation— she's adamant she deserves that much. After all, she put her heart and soul into her marriage. She was a loving and caring wife, not overly bossy, understanding and patient; she never threw away his favorite raggedy T-shirt, even though she was tempted many times. Her adolescent dream had been to find her Prince Charming, a love that would not depart her … and she believed she had found him. He was considerate and never demeaned her, though he made fun of her in jest. Although he wasn't amorous, he had his unique kind of affection. She recalls the time she was bedridden and delirious with an infection. Instead of sleeping on the couch, he slept on the floor next to the bed for six days to keep watch over her through the nights. Her thoughts meander to the time they bought the house, shortly after they wed; as is the custom, he carried her over the threshold, knocking her head gently on the doorframe. They laughed incessantly, and when their laughter subsided, he looked at her and said, "you and me, always." She snaps out of her reflections, and the reality of her loneliness subdues the slight grin prompted by her pleasant memories.

She's thought about moving house but remains in waiting, holding onto a faint hope that one day he'll return, pleading to reunite. And to give her the closure she so desperately desires. If he does, she still hasn't settled on whether she would take him back. One part of her screams *NO WAY*, to avoid a repeat heartbreak. The other part of her yearns to feel validated. She plays the moment over in her mind: as she opens the door and he's standing there. She's compiled a long list of questions. *What did I do wrong? What could I have done better? What didn't you like about me?* That's only the beginning. All her questions center on her being the problem. She's not really conscious that she sees herself as the reason he walked out on her.

Ms. Davis sits motionless in her armchair, gazing blankly ahead while unrestrained thoughts play out in her mind. Her deep thought is broken by the beep of an alarm, signaling a new hour. She turns her head toward the side table and grabs a photo frame. It's from her wedding day. She stares at it apathetically; a quiet tear falls from her eye. After putting the frame back, she reaches beneath the table. She pulls out an unopened bottle of whiskey and a glass. She pours herself a drink and gulps it down, closes her eyes, and drops her head back on to the headrest. Glass in one hand, bottle of whiskey in the other.

Stan, the delivery driver, is making his afternoon deliveries. He pulls up out the front of Ms. Davis' house. New to the job, he took over from the long-serving Mr.

Henjack only two months ago when he retired. It didn't take him long to notice Ms. Davis' reclusive lifestyle and antisocial manner. He grabs her standard weekly order from the back of his van, which always includes a bottle of *Wittman's Whiskey*, and walks up to her front door.

"Curtains closed as usual," he mumbles to himself. He knocks on the front door. Ms. Davis is asleep with a half-empty bottle of whiskey in her hand and an empty glass in the other. Startled by the sudden noise, she looks around dazedly, before realizing someone is at the door. She places the bottle and glass on the side table, slowly and steadily rising from her brief slumber, leaning on the armrest to gain her balance, then shuffles to the door. Stan would have knocked twice by now with any other customer. But he's learned not to do that with Ms. Davis, not unless he wants another verbal rebuke.

She opens the door. Bleary-eyed, scruffy hair, unkempt clothes.

"Good afternoon, Ms. Davis. I have your weekly delivery." He holds up the box of groceries. Nonresponsive, she hastily grabs the box from him and places it on a table near the door. Stan interrupts as she's about to close the door on him.

"Ms. Davis …" She stops and regards him with a stern gaze. He continues. "I've been delivering groceries to you for a little while now … and if you don't mind me asking, what's a lady like yourself doing holed up in her home?"

"I do mind you asking," she says abruptly, closing the door in his face. Only a little surprised, he walks back to his van, shaking his head, and sighs.

"Such a shame."

Ms. Davis slouches back down in her armchair. Grabs the bottle of whiskey and fills her glass. She has a few more hours to get through before her next shift begins. She squanders her days in this self-imposed, unmotivated vacuum. The need to understand why her husband rejected and abandoned her for someone else has become a gnawing obsession that she can't turn off. She turns on the television to drown out the incessant thoughts. The distraction is hardly able to capture her attention; the thoughts are merely shifted to her mind's periphery. It's not long before an image or a phrase sparks some memory. Within seconds, the recollection invades the main screen of her mind. What seems like minutes morph into hours of deep contemplation, rousing visceral angst inside her. She becomes most emotional in the evening twilight hour, just before she heads off to work. That's when she came home to find that her husband had left her. In this hour of torment, without consciously choosing to do so, she has established a weeping ritual. In particular, she muses on what life would be like if he was still around. She looks again at the picture frame on the side table. She grabs it and brings it closer, remembering how happy she was that day. As she gazes at the photograph, increasing resentment rises within. In a sudden fit of rage, she throws the photo frame across the room with such force that she falls forward onto the floor on her knees. Crouched on the floor, gasping and sobbing uncontrollably, she is frustrated with herself, with him, and with what her life has become.

∞

Amanda meanders through the town center, window gazing at whatever takes her interest. She derives a certain serenity from strolling home after a shift in the commencing evening hour; the bustle of the day winds down, and the fading sun offers a soothing ambience. She notices a young mother struggling to manage her three children. A baby boy crying in the pram, a toddler tugging on mummy's arm vying for attention, and a young school-aged girl running around chasing a butterfly. The mother calls out.

"Charlotte, honey, stay near me."

The girl is lost in her own world, focused on following the butterfly. The young mother tends to her baby, trying to pacify him while also giving the toddler the attention he craves. She turns around to check on her daughter who is now perilously close to the traffic.

"Charlotte," she calls, while rocking the baby. Then, "Charlotte!" She shouts in terror—the child is one step away from venturing into oncoming traffic. By this time, Amanda is among them. She leaps to grab Charlotte just before she steps onto the road. The terrified mother breathes a huge sigh of relief.

"Thank you so much," she says to Amanda as she brings the girl to her mother.

"You sure do have your hands full," says Amanda.

"Tell me about it."

"A blessing, though, I'm sure." The mother smiles and nods in confirmation.

"Do you have any children?"

Amanda is troubled by the question. It's the first time anyone has ever asked her that.

"Ahh … no, I don't …" She looks down in confusion. "I mean, I had …" She fumbles, unsure how to respond. Awkwardly, the mother realizes she may have opened up a past wound.

"I'm so sorry," she says. "I shouldn't have asked that question."

"No … no …" Amanda does her best to shrug it off. "That's fine … have a lovely evening." The mother looks on with concern as Amanda caresses the young girl's head and walks away.

Her home is a short stroll from town, but she sometimes takes the longer route. There's a church a couple of streets out of the way, which she sometimes visits. It's become a routine over the years. She tentatively makes her way through the small lobby toward the doors leading to the nave. She partially opens the door and sticks her head through to see if it's empty. If there's a service or a gathering, she'll hastily leave. But it's usually empty besides one or two others sitting there in the silence. She slides in, eyes cast downward, and makes her way to her usual seat in the pew furthest from the altar. She feels unworthy of approaching any closer. She ponders the incident with the mother and her children. It has intensified her already ingrained self-condemnation. She closes her eyes and bows her head, sinking lower and lower, until her neck can't give any further, chin touching her chest. After some time, laboriously, she lifts her head. Afraid to open her eyes, she breathes a remorseful sigh and whispers with a quiver, "please forgive me." Her head falls again like a lead weight, and a flood of remorse pools underneath her eyelids. Droplets escape from the inner corners of her eyes. She spends a few minutes in silent contemplation, hoping that one of these days, she'll be free of the enduring guilt. Then, she places her hands on the back of the seat in front to lift herself up. Every day, she drags the self-inflicted weight. But never once has she prayed to be released from the pain. Amanda believes she must bear the heartache as punishment for the rest of her life. Rather, she seeks only a sense of forgiveness. She makes her way toward the door, eyes cast down until she leaves the church lobby.

After a refreshing shower, Amanda pours hot water from the kettle into a mug, igniting the chamomile aroma of the tea bag. The soothing brew helps her to sleep, and she needs it tonight especially. She heads to the backyard as she does every night before bed. She opens the sliding door leading to the small patio and leans against the doorframe. Looking up at the stars, she takes a couple of deep breaths. She then looks down at a seven-year-old blue poppy in the middle of her garden. She walks over to the plant and places her mug on the nearby bench. She bends down and tends to it, grabs a watering can and waters its base and lightly drizzles the top. It's almost the season for the plant to produce its flowers: vivid, blue crepe-like petals with little yellow-tipped antlers reaching out from the center. There's a sign in the ground: *In memory of my child.* There's space for a name to be written, but it remains blank. She caresses the leaves and, looking closer, finds a few buds that signal the imminent birth of a new season. She grabs her mug, sits on the bench and admires the plant until she finishes her tea.

∞

Doctor Fletcher exits the hospital toward the car park, briefcase in hand. He gets into his car, places the briefcase on the front passenger seat, and drives off. A flashing light on the dash grabs his attention; the gas tank is almost empty. He turns into the next gas station he sees. While filling the tank, he stares forlornly into the distance. He then gazes at the ring on his left hand perched on the roof of his car. His wedding band. He hasn't taken it off in seven years. He lifts his hand and, with his thumb, caresses the ring. His concentration is interrupted by the thud of the full gas tank. He places the gas nozzle back on the pump and heads to the station office to pay. While waiting in line, he grabs two white roses. He hurries back to the car in the dwindling sunlight and drives out of town onto Burkwood Highway.

He makes the solemn quarter-hour drive several times a year, on birthdays, anniversaries, and special occasions. No sound from the car radio, no gust of the rushing breeze from an open window. He wants the undisturbed silence so he can be alone with his memories. His thoughts meander to the occasion of his visit. Today, he recalls the few birthdays he celebrated with his daughter, still vivid memories etched onto his mind. He turns off the highway into the street that leads to Burkwood Cemetery. He parks the car near the entrance and grabs the roses sitting on the briefcase. The last remnants of sunlight linger. Every time he visits, he wrestles with an array of emotions that intensify during the short walk from the entrance to their resting place. He grits his teeth, gaze fixed on the worn grass pathway. The weight of regret crushes his chest, his eyes fill with grief, the rose stems bear the brunt of his tightly clenched fist. He reaches their headstones and stares on blankly. He grabs a rose and bends down on one knee, reaches over, and places the rose at the foot of the large headstone.

"Miss you so much, Soph." He caresses the face of her headstone. His lower lip starts to quiver. He turns to the smaller headstone. "Ruby." His sorrow intensifies. "Happy Birthday, sweetheart … ten years today." He places the other white rose at the foot of her headstone and strokes her name etched on the marble. "You would have been such a beautiful young girl." He sinks to the ground and lays there, wiping his incessant tears on the sleeve of his coat. He mutters apologies profusely through the tears and groans. "I'm sorry … I'm so sorry … it's all my fault. I should have paid attention." He sobs louder.

"I miss you so much."

Doctor Fletcher rubs his weary eyes; the glare from the computer screen is beginning to irritate him. When he can't sleep, he turns to work, which usually fatigues him eventually. However, his restlessness is amplified on days that represent special family occasions. They evoke specific thoughts about what the day would be like if Sophie and Ruby were here to celebrate. The images ebb and flow throughout the night at will. He attempts to settle himself and gather focus; however, in his weariness, his concentration trails off repeatedly into reveries until he becomes aware and snaps himself out of it. Once again, he gains composure, determined not to allow the images to rule his thoughts. He rummages through a pile of documents on his disorganized desk. He takes a pile of papers to move them elsewhere, then suddenly stops. He's uncovered a photograph he took of Sophie and Ruby, from her third birthday. Placing the pile down, he picks up the photo. He imagines it's the present day. He's sitting at the dining room table. Plates and cutlery have been set for three. Birthday decorations and presents adorn the table. A ten-year-old Ruby is with him.

"I love you, sweetheart," he says admiringly. Ruby tilts her head and smiles. "You've grown up to be such a smart and beautiful young lady." As he speaks, Sophie walks in with a birthday cake. "Woah," he says, "here it is!"

"It's your favorite," Sophie says as she places the cake in front of Ruby. Vanilla cake with chocolate icing, candles with "1" and "0" already lit, side by side.

"Close your eyes and make a wish, sweetie," he says.

"You have to close your eyes too," Ruby says.

"Okay, okay." They all close their eyes. "After three … and tell us when you're done. One … two … three." A puff of wind and the smell of blown-out candles lingers in the brief silence.

"All done," Ruby confirms. He opens his eyes to look at Ruby. She's a three-year-old again, looking back at him. He snaps out of his daydream. There, he was content—it felt so real to him. His contented smile fades to sadness as he comes back down to reality. His eyes well up, still gazing at the photograph he's holding. He gently strokes the photo, wishing he could hold them again. He puts the photograph down and opens the top desk drawer. Thomas pulls out a bottle of pills, pours a few into his hand and chucks them into his mouth. He grabs the glass of water on his desk and gulps it all down. He leans back into his chair, closes his eyes and sighs.

∞

Amanda wipes down the patio tables with one hand while holding plates in the other. Playful noise fills the air, as is often the case after the children receive their morning tea. The children are exuberant, some chasing each other in the yard, while others kick the soccer ball around. Except Max. He sits on his own in one corner of the patio; it's become a routine during play breaks. He used to be invited to join them but he never accepted an invitation. He maintains his toughened *I-don't-need-anyone* exterior. Now, the other children leave him be and don't bother to ask anymore. He wants them to keep asking, though. It makes him feel wanted. Each day that passes without an invite intensifies his agitation. He perches himself in the same spot every day, so they'll know where to find him, waiting in expectation for anyone to come by and ask him to play.

On this day, he nears boiling point. His leg shakes nervously and he chews his fingernails, watching with disdain the other children having fun and laughing. He thinks they're laughing at him, and the sound of their laughter sparks painful memories of his parents laughing and mocking him. Abruptly, he heads to his room to escape the joyful noise. He sits heavily on the edge of his bed, hands and teeth clenched, breathing deeply, then grabs his exercise book and a pen. Aggressively, he scribbles, *no one loves me*. Another addition to the self-deprecating words saturating the pages. Retracing the words until the page tears under the force of the pen. He stops and breathes out a long sigh. The release of this angst onto the page relieves the tension a little. Calmly, he places the exercise book beside him. His thoughts turn to his parents. He often thinks about going back to live with them—but not if they're stuck in their old ways. No one ever tells him anything about his parents; he has to ask. It's been a little over a year since he last asked about them. At that time, he was told they had improved but still remained in a rehabilitation program. He wonders why it's taking so long for them to recover. *Wouldn't they want to get better for me, to have me back?* He's curious to know if they at least think of him and ask about him. He heads back to the patio and shuffles nervously toward Amanda. He knows she's in touch with Child Protective Services regularly and is familiar with each child's background. She's sitting on the patio watching the children, but she notices his movement in her peripheral vision.

"Hey Max, everything okay?" She notices his uncharacteristically humble posture.

"Miss Grace," he says politely, gazing downward, fiddling with the hem of his shirt. "Um … are my parents doing okay?"

"Yeah," she says, with an upbeat tone. "They're living independently now and continue to get the help they need."

He nods, then looks at her. "Do they … ask about me?"

She opens her mouth to speak but hesitates, trying to formulate an appropriate response. She's asked Child Protective Services many times over the years if the parents want to see Max, but the usual response is that "they haven't mentioned anything." From her experience, she guesses that the parents have all but disowned the child. Her heart breaks for him; she knows that he needs parental love more than any of the other children there. She responds cautiously. "They're really focused on getting better, Max. I'm sure they think about you, though."

His head drops. He knows what she means. Embarrassed, he wishes he hadn't asked. Filled with compassion, she places her hand on his shoulder.

"You okay, Max?"

His toughened exterior returns and he blurts out, "I'm fine", before hurrying back to his room to be alone.

Max lies awake among the other boys slumbering in the room. He can't get an inch of sleep. His thoughts have been running unbridled since his interaction with Amanda, haunted by the confirmed reality that his parents don't want him. Until now, he'd held hope that all the nasty things they'd ever said to him were their addictions talking. But now that they're sober, and still maintain their aversion to him, he's lost all hope. A recurring thought weighs heavily on his mind. *If my own parents don't want me, who else will?* He's come to learn that as an orphaned child ages, particularly into their teenage years, they're less likely to be wanted—and therefore not adopted. He embraces himself in the fetal position, rocking back and forth.

∞

On his daily dawn laneway raid, Bruce peers into a dumpster. He knows into which ones the surrounding restaurants and cafés dump their leftovers at night. Navigating the garbage bags, he opens them one by one in search of some breakfast. He reaches into a bag, swatting away the non-edible items to get to a half-eaten piece of toast with avocado. He pulls it out and picks off a bottle top stuck to the avocado. He sniffs the piece of toast several times. Content that it has passed the smell test, he takes a nibble to assess the taste. He nods his head in confirmation and takes a larger bite. Satisfied with his morning find, he turns into Downman Road as the world around him wakes to the daily grind. He hobbles along, eyes down, hands tucked into his well-worn overcoat. He hears a passerby mumble a snide remark; he's unsure of what was said exactly but knows he heard the word "lazy." Another person paces toward him, a businessman reading a message on his phone. Bruce looks up and stops to avoid bumping into the man. The man suddenly stops a hand length shy of Bruce. He jumps back, offended by his presence. "Go away!" He shakes his head and hastily walks around him. A woman passes him by, eyes wide open but staring straight ahead. He's accustomed to that look: the one where you know they've noticed you but pretend not to see you. He hangs his head and continues to hobble along. Not a day passes where he doesn't receive a judgmental word, gaze, or attitude. The years of condemning stares, sneering remarks, and obvious evasion have built up a stubborn, near-impenetrable wall around his heart. An attitude solidified by the lack of a single open heart or hand of grace extended to him. He adopts the consistent rejection of others as his justification for avoiding relationship with others, an excuse to protect himself from further abandonment.

Bruce walks off the main road into Doves Crescent, which leads to Doves Park, named after the doves that have nested there for over a century. He arrives at his favorite park bench. At just the right time of the morning, the sun hits the bench with a comfortable, warm touch. It reminds him of his late wife's hand on his cheek. Every day, he pulls out his only photograph of her, the one from their wedding day, and spends a few moments reminiscing. The park bench is usually empty, but today someone is sitting on the end. Bruce approaches the bench quietly and sits at the opposite end, so as not to trouble the man. Busily scrolling his cell phone, he doesn't notice Bruce. Bruce takes a couple of deep breathes as he waits for the sun to hit that special spot. The man then looks across at him. Bruce notices the sudden jerk of the man's head in his peripheral vision, looks across, and acknowledges him with a slight nod.

The man looks down at him, wrinkles his nose, jumps off the seat and walks away. Bruce sighs. His acknowledgment of the other man, a rare moment of vulnerability, is met by yet another rejection. The moment brings to his mind all the times he's been told to "move on," "you can't stay here," or "can you please leave." Not one to stay where he's not wanted, he gets up and hobbles away forlornly.

Bruce adjusts his coat collar, pulling it up to keep out the bitter nightly chill. He walks by a takeaway shop closing up for the night, then decides to wait on the curb out front of the shop. He doesn't usually interact with shop owners, but tonight his stomach growls intensely from hunger pain, more so than usual. The lights are off, and the owner walks out to lock the door from the outside. Bruce approaches the owner.
"Leftovers'?"
"Got nothing tonight."
Disappointed, Bruce nods and wanders off. He walks past a dark alley and notices a fresh stack of plump garbage bags glistening under the laneway light. He walks toward the garbage bags and arranges them as comfortable as possible to rest for the night. Lowering himself carefully onto the garbage bags, he wriggles into a cozy position. He pulls his beanie down to cover more

of his face and crosses his arms tightly to keep warm. Fog
rises from every breath as he settles for the night.

Touched by Grace

My grace is sufficient for you,
for my power is made perfect in weakness.

– 2 Corinthians 12:9 (NIV)

The welcome warmth follows the morning sun, brightening the patio after an unseasonably chilly night. A cacophony of banter fills the air as the children eat their morning tea. Amanda sits alone, deep in thought as she scours paperwork, but still looking up periodically to check that all is well with the children. Engrossed in her work, she doesn't notice Bruce digging through garbage cans outside the fence on the far side of the yard. Manny, however, notices the distant movement. It takes his attention away from the conversion he's listening in on. The man looks familiar—unkempt silver hair, aged hobble, and ragged overcoat—and he realizes it's the same man he saw the other day on the way to the hospital, out front of the café. Manny looks down at the remaining half sandwich on his plate. He picks up the plate and walks toward Bruce. The other children don't notice him getting up, and neither does Amanda. He reaches the vertical steel fence, grabs the sandwich, and sticks his arm through the fence. Bruce doesn't notice, his head inside a garage can, trying to discern what might be edible. However, he doesn't find anything. Upon pulling his head back, the little arm poking through the fence, holding half a sandwich, takes him by surprise. He looks at Manny. Manny waves the sandwich to suggest he take it. Tentatively, Bruce reaches for it. He cradles the sandwich in both hands like a treasure, before slowly bringing it to his mouth, closing his eyes and joyfully taking a mouthful. He gives Manny an appreciative smile and nod. *Thank you.* His watery eyes gleam with gratitude, not so much for the sandwich, but simply for noticing him there.

"You're not forgotten. Jesus loves you and he knows who you are." Bruce is taken aback by Manny's comment.

"He does?"

Manny nods his head with a big approving smile. Bruce's face lights up as though he's received the greatest revelation he's ever heard. He looks up joyfully as he walks away, his face gazing skyward. Manny watches as he walks off. Amanda looks up briefly and does a double take. There's an empty seat, and she realizes it was where Manny was sitting. She figures he must be in the yard; he couldn't be inside because she's sitting by the sliding door and would have noticed if someone walked by her. She places the paperwork on the table and gets up so she can view the whole yard. She scans the area and finally spots him by the fence, peering out into the street. By this time, Bruce has disappeared out of sight. She tells the other children to finish their breakfast and to go inside, then heads toward Manny.

"Manny." He turns around to look at her. "What are you doing?" He remains silent. She grabs him by the hand and pulls him away from the fence. She looks out to see what he might be looking at but can't see anything unusual. "C'mon Manny … time to go inside." She leads him back by the hand.

The children are seated at their tables ready for the morning lesson, exercise books in front of them.

"We're going to do a little exercise. Open your book to a new page," Amanda says. A chorus of page rustling ensues.

"I want you to write a few nice things about yourself. It could be what you think of yourself, or it could be something your good at, or it could be something nice someone has said to you." Several children get straight to writing, while others ponder, gazing at the ceiling. Manny leans over to help Abby write something.

After several minutes, Amanda gets their attention.

"Okay children, I'd love to hear some of the things you have written, but … before I do, I just want to say something nice about *all* of you." The children listen intently, anticipating the nice thing she's going to say. "Every single one of you is priceless. There is no one like you in the world. You are one of a kind … and that's the truth." The children smile, swing their legs in delight, and sit up straight, enlivened by her uplifting comments. She continues.

"Rosie. Tell me something you've written about yourself?"

"I have pretty hair."

"Very good. You do have pretty hair … wish I had hair like yours."

"Kevin. What did you write?"

"I'm a fast runner."

"Yes, you are. I've seen you zip around the yard. Maybe one day you'll compete in the Olympics." He nods in excitement.

"Ok … how about—" Abby interrupts by sticking up her hand.

"Um, Miss Grace, I write something too."

Amanda smiles. "Okay Abby, what did you write?"

She squirms in her chair. "Um … um …. Manny says I'm precious." Amanda tilts her head adoringly.

"Yes, you are very precious, Abby. And don't ever forget it."

Amanda turns her gaze toward Max. "Max, what did you write?" Max doesn't respond right away. Annoyed, he stares at his closed exercise book.

"I didn't write anything good." He leans forward, folded arms covering his exercise book to conceal what he has written.

"Surely, you could have thought of something?"

"I've got nothing." He raises his voice.

Amanda notices his agitation. "Okay Max … you need a little more time, that's fine." Shifting the attention away from him, she speaks to all the children. "Okay kiddies, its playtime. Be sure to put your exercise books away in your rooms." The children scramble to their rooms, doing as Amanda instructed. Manny places his exercise book on his bedside table, which he shares with Max. A few moments later, Max enters the room and, from a distance, throws his exercise book on the same bedside table. He doesn't see that it knocks Manny's book off the table and underneath the bed.

∞

Manny retreats to his room and turns on the table lamp. He sits on the edge of his bed and grabs Max's exercise book, believing that it's his. He opens it to write something positive about the day but is confronted with angry and demeaning words. *No one loves me … I'm a mistake.*

"Who wrote this?" Manny says under his breath. He flicks through the pages, realizing that it's not his book. Max walks into the room, and Manny looks up at him in fright. Max notices his sudden look of shock and peers down at the exercise book Manny is holding open. Max sees his own handwriting.

"What are you doing with my book?!" He charges toward Manny, growing increasingly upset. "Give it back!" He snatches the book from his grasp. Startled, Manny tries to explain.

"Sorry Max … I … I thought it was my book."

"You're gonna pay for this." Max tightly clutches his exercise book close to his chest, breathing heavily, gritting his teeth, on the verge of an outburst. "Get out of here!"

Seeing how distraught Max is, Manny jumps off his bed to hurry out of the room. He stops in the doorway and turns around to face Max.

"You are loved, Max … God loves you."

"Oh yeah?" Max's rage spills out. "If God loves me so much, where was he when I needed him? Why didn't he answer my prayers? Why didn't he stop—" He pauses mid-sentence, not wanting to divulge any more about his past. He turns his back to Manny.

"He did hear your prayers, Max. Sometimes bad things happen to those who don't deserve it."

"Well … maybe I did deserve it. Maybe I shouldn't have been born."

"That's not true, Max. You wouldn't have been born if God didn't have a plan for your life." Max is struck by this. Manny adds, "I love you too, Max," then walks away to give him some space.

Max's demeanor shifts from anger to confusion, as he begins to question how he views himself.

∞

Amanda finishes washing the dishes after dinner while the children wind down in the evening glow of the television. She leaves the dishes in the rack to dry and heads to her desk to finalize a case file before her shift ends. The phone rings.

"Amanda speaking."

"Amanda, hi, it's Doctor Fletcher."

"Oh, hi Doctor."

"Calling to let you know I have the results of Manny's latest test. Are you able to stop by tomorrow morning?"

"I can't, sorry, I'll be on my shift."

"Oh, well, I can pop over on my lunch break, if that suits you?"

"If it's not too much trouble, that would be great, thank you Doctor. You're a lifesaver … in more ways than one." They both giggle.

"Okay, I'll see you tomorrow."

"See you then." She hangs up the phone with a big smile on her face. She turns around and sees Manny near her, staring up at her. Startled by his sudden appearance, she asks, "Manny, is everything okay?"

He nods. "Doctor Fletcher makes you happy." He runs back to his seat on the couch. Amanda laughs in bewilderment, mumbling to herself. "What?"

∞

Doctor Fletcher enters the orphanage.

"Hello … hello?" There seems to be no one around.

Amanda pops her head in from the outside patio.

"Take a seat, Doctor," she says, indicating with her hand the seat on the other side of the desk. "I'll be with you in a sec."

Doctor Fletcher takes his seat as Amanda comes inside.

"Sorry Doctor, thanks for dropping by."

"Not a problem."

Just as she sits down, Abby shouts from the yard.

"Miss Grace, Max hurting me."

"Max!" She shouts back, remaining still and hoping her warning will calm the situation.

"Miss Grace!" Abby shouts louder. Amanda sighs and excuses herself.

"Excuse me, Doctor, I'll be right back."

"Do what you need to do." Doctor Fletcher lifts his hands to imply there's no explanation needed.

Amanda is outside investigating the situation when Manny walks in.

"Hey Doc, are you here for me?"

"Hey Manny, yes … I am here for you."

"Well… what's the verdict, Doc?"

Doctor Fletcher looks down in dismay and hesitates. "… Manny …"

"It's okay, Doc," Manny interrupts him, placing his hand on his shoulder. "I know it's not looking good." Doctor Fletcher smiles at him with compassion.

"Doc, can I ask you a question?"

"Sure, go ahead."

"The last time we met, you said you used to believe in God. What did you mean?"

After a moment of deliberation, Doctor Fletcher explains.

"I lost the people I loved the most."

Manny ponders this.

"The tragedies of life can make you feel like all hope is gone. But it's in those times you need to cling to hope the most. In time, God will get you through the tough times and give you the comfort and healing you need. The answer to your healing might be right in front of you, but because you're focused on the pain, you can miss it."

The doctor listens intently as Amanda walks back in, carrying Abby in her arms.

"Sorry about that, Doctor." She puts Abby down near Doctor Fletcher and grabs a tissue from her desk to dry Abby's tears and running nose.

He smiles at Abby with admiration. "Who's this little angel?"

"This is Abby. She's two and a half years old, and … as Manny says, she's precious." Abby rubs one eye with her fist while looking at Doctor Fletcher with her other eye.

"I'm precious," Abby repeats in a croaky voice.

"You are very precious, Abby," he replies.

"Manny, can you please take Abby outside and look after her?" He nods and takes Abby by the hand.

"Let's go, Abby." He leads her outside. Abby turns to Doctor Fletcher and waves.

"B-bye."

He waves back with a big smile.

Amanda takes a seat. "She really wants to be a part of a real family one day," she says.

"She's adorable. She reminds me of …" The doctor trails off, and his countenance changes. Suddenly filled with empathy, Amanda finishes his sentence.

"… Of your daughter … What was her name?"

"Ruby … And my wife's name was Sophie. If I just took another way home that night, or if I was more vigilant, they'd still be here."

"You shouldn't blame yourself for things outside your control." There's a brief moment of silence before Amanda opens up to him a little.

"And then there are the things you *can* control." He looks up at her, wondering what she means. Amanda's expression changes, and he looks on in confusion, waiting for her to continue.

"In senior year," she explains, "I got pregnant. My then-boyfriend wanted nothing to do with me, so I was on my own. I made the decision—" She pauses mid-sentence, overcome with a powerful feeling of regret. "To stop it."

"And you've felt guilty ever since?"

Amanda doesn't answer the question. She didn't need to—the answer was written all over her face.

"You were young and confused … I'm sure you did what you thought was the best choice at the time."

"Still doesn't change the fact that I chose the fate of a life." There's a brief silence. "You know," she muses, "a wise little man once said to me, 'you have to forgive yourself before you can put the past behind you, and move on'." They both reflect on this for a moment.

"He's a special kid," says the doctor. "Speaking of Manny, I have his results." He holds up the documents. "Unfortunately, as expected, his situation has not improved. However, it is stable."

"It's amazing. He knows any day now might be his last, but he's so positive and he appreciates life more than most. He deserves to be in a loving family, but because of his condition, no one will adopt him." While Amanda is speaking, Manny walks back in, hand-in-hand with Abby. He overhears their conversation.

"That's okay," he intervenes. "I like it here. Besides, I don't want to take the spot of another child who needs a mummy and daddy." He looks down at Abby. "C'mon Abby, let's get your book."

Amanda and Doctor Fletcher look at each other, awed by his selflessness.

"See what I mean?" She says.

"I've never known a child so selfless … what a great kid," says the doctor as his phone beeps. He reads the message. "Ah, I've got to get back to the hospital. I appreciate your time, Amanda."

"Not at all, *thank you* for coming by, Doctor." Amanda escorts him to the door. "And thank you for listening … I haven't opened up about my past to anyone … ever," she explains.

"I don't speak about my family so openly as I have with you … and please… call me Thom." She smiles and nods. "Okay … bye."

∞

It's pitch dark at the orphanage, just the way Ms. Davis likes it. She spends her hours of solitude in endless moping catharsis, devoid of light and people. The only interaction she has during her shift occurs in the few hours before the children go to sleep, and when her shift ends at dawn, as Amanda takes over. Like every other night, the only illumination comes from the low-light yellow glow of a desk lamp. The eerie silence is broken by the lone beep of a desk clock indicating the midnight hour. Wearily, Manny sits up in his bed; he needs to use the bathroom. When he's done, he starts heading back to his bed but stops in the hallway. A faint distant sound grabs his attention. Someone is sobbing. Tentatively, he follows the sound and discovers Ms. Davis at her desk. She's weeping, staring at a picture frame. She doesn't see him in the darkness, standing in the distance. He slowly moves closer. Startled by the small figure approaching in the darkness, she quickly puts the picture frame face down, hides her glass in the drawer, and shoves the bottle of whiskey in her handbag. Annoyed by the unwelcome interruption, she quietly snaps.

"What are you doing here? Go back to bed."

Manny stops just inside the edge of the lamp's glow. "Sorry, Ms. Davis. I heard you crying … are you okay?"

"Yes, yes. Just go back to bed." She hastily wipes at the tears beneath her eyes.

He moves closer to her. She's surprised by his lack of compliance and his boldness. Usually, the children don't hesitate to obey her commands. He places his hand on her hand. She gulps, bewildered. The first act of affection she's felt in years. Not quite sure what to do, she attempts to speak but is lost for words. She stares at his hand on her hand with unease.

"The hurt will overwhelm you if you keep holding on to it," he says. "You try to take the pain away, but nothing works. In this life, you may never know why things happen the way they do. But when you forgive and let go, you'll be free. Then the hate and the pain can turn to love and peace."

A passive kind of fear emanates from Ms. Davis' wide eyes. She remains still, in stunned silence apart from a slight tremble. A gasp breaks the silence, the release of an emotional pressure valve. A flood submerges her eyes, and a cascade of droplets falls.

However, what once were tears of sorrow are now tears of liberation, the release of many years of anguish and heartbreak. She senses a visceral weight of self-condemnation lifting from her heart; she takes a deep breath, then joyfully exhales a sense of peace. Each teardrop represents a burden she had collected and held fast over the last seven years. Manny's words dawn on her, an epiphany. For the first time, she understands that she's been living a life of self-imposed bondage. She allowed her wounded heart to fester into a cesspool of anger, misery, and guilt, shut all others out and built a wall around her heart within.

Ms. Davis looks at Manny with appreciation, for beginning to awaken a hopeful new life. He lifts his arms to give her a hug. She hesitates at first; the remnants of her past life still linger. However, she overcomes this brief hesitation, slowly leans in and softly hugs him. Feeling steadily more at ease, she squeezes him tighter, releasing an deep sigh of relief. They pull back from the embrace. He places his hand on her cheek.

"It will get better, Ms. Davis."

She nods in agreement, tears still raining, mouth quivering, too overjoyed to speak. Manny walks back to his room. She watches him disappearing into the darkness. She is overwhelmed by the feeling of rebirth. She closes her eyes and steadily breathes in and out, regaining her composure. She mumbles to herself repeatedly, *I forgive*. She leans back in her chair; she laughs and cries at the same time, relieved to be free of the burden that had enslaved her for so long. She looks down at the glass and bottle of whiskey, grabs them, and heads to the kitchen sink. She pours out the contents. She walks back to her desk and grabs the picture frame she was staring at: a photo from her wedding day she had been carrying in her handbag. She stares at it one last time before letting it slide from her hand and into the waste bin. She sits back down in relief, smiling with contentment. "Thank you, thank you," she whispers.

∞

Amanda enters the orphanage.

"Good morning, Amanda. How are you this beautiful day?"

Ms. Davis' uncharacteristic greeting shocks Amanda to a standstill. She looks around—thinking, *what's going on?*—not quite sure how to respond.

"Um … ah … I'm good." She's unsure if that's the answer Ms. Davis wanted to hear.

"Great to hear."

"How are *you* going? Is everything okay, Ms. Davis?" Amanda asks in confusion.

Ms. Davis chuckles as she prepares to leave. On her way out, she faces Amanda and places her hands on her shoulders.

"Things couldn't be any better," she says. Then she heads out the door. Amanda watches her leave, still confused.

The Healing Road

Heal me, Lord, and I will be healed;
save me and I will be saved,
for you are the one I praise.

– Jeremiah 17:14 (NIV)

Amanda pulls into the parking lot of the Night-2-Day Supermarket. Hers is one of a few cars scattered throughout the parking lot. The pulsing buzz and flicker of a fluorescent light in the foyer greet her as she grabs a basket. Subconsciously, she hums along to a classic 90s ballad playing in the background as she browses the products on the shelves. The staff intentionally select the Late Night Love Ballads radio station during these late-night hours to accommodate the majority of shoppers, singles in their mid-twenties to late thirties. The supermarket employees affectionately call the shoppers of this time "the lonely-heart-ers." Amanda meanders leisurely into an aisle. There, at the other end, stands Doctor Fletcher. He's examining items on the shelf, unaware of her presence. She walks up to him.

"You couldn't sleep either?" He looks up in surprise, but the sight of her makes him smile.

"What better activity than late night shopping to put you to sleep … right?"

"Oh. I hear you … so exhausting!" They giggle.

"How's Manny doing?"

"He's going okay. The other day he felt tired quite suddenly, but after some rest, he felt better." Doctor Fletcher nods.

"That will happen with someone in his condition." Silence ensues, and he shifts his attention to a bottle of Reginio tomato sauce. He contemplates changing the conversation to something more personal but he's unsure if this is the time or place. He looks back at Amanda, hoping to gain some sign of approval. She's gazing at a packet of Reginio pasta. She grabs it, holds it up, looks at him with a cheeky grin.

"Penne for your thoughts?" He laughs; they place the items back on the shelf and continue to shop together.

"I want to thank you again for listening the other day. I felt such a sense of relief talking to you," he says.

"I felt the same way."

"It's a bit like we're each other's therapists."

"Spoken like a true doctor," Amanda says. "I'd prefer to say … we're each other's shoulders to lean on."

He nods in agreement. "That's a much better way to put it. A shared comfort. Shared grief."

"Yeah … a grief that's anchored us … like we're stuck in that one moment."

"Mmm." He nods. "Those moments won't ever be forgotten, but as for being anchored by them … I think that might be a choice…" He sighs in resignation. "I want to move on from the heartache, but I don't know if anything can ease the pain. It's like there's a domineering part of me that won't let me move on.

"You know … Manny told me once, the comfort to your pain can be right in front of you. He said you can be so blinded by the hurt you miss the very thing you need to help you heal."

He ponders her remark. "Huh, Manny said the same thing to me the other day."

They reach the self-service checkout and scan their items.

Doctor Fletcher pauses—a moment of clarity—before continuing. "What Manny said makes sense. I've been seeing the world so negatively all these years, I hardly notice the beauty anymore."

Amanda listens intently while placing the remaining items in her shopping bag. They grab their bags, deep in thought, and walk slowly toward the parking lot.

"And I guess people live in the past because they're afraid that the good thing they once had will be lost forever. Or maybe… some don't feel like they deserve to move on," she says.

"We speak like we're referring to other people, when really, we're talking about us … aren't we? This is what we've become," the doctor says.

They reach the middle of the parking lot. She turns to face him.

"I hope we can get past our anchors," she says.

"Well, having you as my therapist—" He corrects himself. "—'my shoulder,' certainly helps."

She appreciates the compliment.

"Thank you, Thom, for a *wonderful* shopping experience. I can truly say it's the most enjoyable time I've ever spent grocery shopping," she says, only semi-sarcastically. He smiles in amusement.

"It was enlightening to walk through my …" He looks up, trying to find the right word. "Burdens, with someone."

She nods in agreement. "Well, ah, I'm over there," she says, pointing over her shoulder to indicate where she's parked.

"I'm this way." He motions with his head, indicating that he's parked in the opposite direction. They both hesitate to make the first move, then simultaneously take one small step back.

"Hope to bump into you soon sometime," she adds.

"I hope so … Good night, Amanda." He slowly backs up further toward his car.

"Night, Thom." She backs up too. They hang onto each other's gaze before slowly turning around at the same time.

∞

The children wake to the sound of the breakfast bell. Louisa, a consistent early riser, has been assigned the responsibility of gently shaking awake the heavy sleepers. The children line up outside the bathrooms; after refreshing themselves, they hurry to the patio eating area. Amanda brings out the breakfast meals she's prepared and places them in front of the children. All the children have their breakfast, but she's still holding one last plate. She runs her eyes over the children and realizes Manny is missing.

"Where's Manny?" She asks the children with concern.

"Maybe he's still sleeping," one of the children says with a shrug.

Louisa speaks up. "Nope, he's definitely up."

Amanda rushes inside to Manny's room, but just as she is about to walk in, she stops. Manny is kneeling by his bed, eyes closed, praying. Not wanting to disturb him, she takes a step back, out of sight, but within earshot.

"And God, I pray for Abby, that you will give her a mummy and daddy that will take good care of her. Amen."

His prayer tugs on Amanda's heart. She pokes her head into the room and lightly knocks on the door.

"Manny, breakfast is ready." Startled, he gets up hastily and makes his way to the patio. Amanda follows. One of the children grabs her attention.

"Miss Grace, Abby is sick," she says. Amanda kneels beside Abby.

"What's the matter, sweetie?"

"Tummy … hurts."

"Come on … let's go back to bed." She picks her up and carries her to her bedroom, places her in bed and pulls the covers over her.

"Get some rest, sweetie." She strokes Abby's head gently.

A commotion erupts on the patio. Amanda looks out the door, but she can't discern what's going on. She turns to Abby. "I'll be right back." She rushes out to see what the problem is.

"What's going on out here?" She snaps, annoyed.

"Max threw food at me," says one child.

"He started it," Max responds.

Amanda is exasperated. "Enough! Just eat your breakfast." She grabs the dustpan and cleans up the food strewn across the floor. The phone rings. She sighs in frustration and rushes to answer the phone.

"Hello." She says curtly.

"Hi Amanda, it's Thom … have I got you at a bad time?"

"Oh, hi Thom," she says, rubbing her forehead. "No, it's fine."

"I was just calling to organize Manny's next appointment. Will Tuesday morning be fine?" She barely hears his question, her attention fixed on the children in the patio. Simon has his arm wound back, with a handful of food. He looks through the glass door to check if the coast is clear. Amanda points at him with a disapproving look, then waves her finger at him, as if to say, *don't you dare*. He puts down his arm and places the food back on the plate.

"Amanda?" Doctor Fletcher checks if she's still on the line.

"Sorry … yeah sure, next Tuesday … that will be fine," she says, sounding flustered.

"Are you okay, Amanda?"

"Not really," she sighs. "The children have decided to play with their breakfast instead of eating it, and Abby is sick. It's been a chaotic start to the day."

"I'm free this morning. I can come by and check on Abby, if you like?"

"That would be great," she says with relief. "That will save me having to take her to the doctor. Thank-you so much."

"My pleasure. I'll see you soon."

∞

Doctor Fletcher pokes his head through the doorway, expecting to encounter a ruckus.

"Hi Thom," Amanda says.

The children sit quietly in the lounge area.

"I see you've managed to calm things down."

"It's amazing how Saturday morning cartoon TV can calm children."

He chuckles. "How's Abby?"

"Follow me." Amanda leads the way to Abby's room.

"Abby, sweetie." She kneels beside her. "Doctor Fletcher is here to check on you, is that okay?" Abby gives an approving nod. Amanda moves aside to let him kneel beside her.

"Abby, where are you feeling the pain?"

"Here," she says, about to cry, placing her hands on her stomach.

"Okay … I'm going to feel around your tummy and I want you to tell me if you feel any pain." He lightly pushes down on her lower abdomen. He watches her to

100

see if she reacts, but she remains still. He grabs a popsicle stick and a small flashlight from his bag. "Abby, sweetie, can you open your mouth and say, 'aaaah'?" Abby lets out a lengthy "aaaah," while Doctor Fetcher examines her throat. "Mmm." He contemplates what he sees.

Amanda watches, fiddling with the pendant around her neck, observing his gentle care and concern for Abby. He places his hand on Abby's forehead to check her temperature. "You're a bit warm." He pulls the sheets back over Abby up to her chest. "Okay, we're all done."

"Is she okay, Doctor?"

He stands up. "I think she has a bug, which is causing the slight fever and tummy pain. It's nothing serious. My prescription is rest and fluids until she feels better. If you don't see any improvement in the next two days, let me know."

"I will. Thank you, Doctor."

"No problem." He leans down to grab his bag. As he reaches down, his head nears Abby's face. She sits up a little and kisses him on the forehead.

"Fank you, Doctor," she says.

He's overwhelmed by her act of affection. He raises his hand to his forehead. "You're welcome, precious," he says softly.

Amanda places her hand on her chest, moved by their interaction. They walk out of the room and stop in the hallway together.

Amanda had noticed how affected he was by the kiss.

"Are you okay, Thom?"

He remains silent, lost in a memory of the last kiss he received from his daughter. It was on his forehead, the night of the accident.

"Abby reminds me so much of …" His voice trails off with a quiver.

"I know," she interrupts, "I know." She places her hand on his arm for comfort.

"She's such a sweet girl. I hope she finds a wonderful family," he says.

"If you need to talk, I'm free this evening," she says.

"That would be nice … but I have shift. I'd like to take you up on that offer another time."

"Sure … anytime."

∞

Ms. Davis wriggles awake to the chime of the 3:00 pm alarm. She sits up in bed and stretches her arms in the air, moving her body from side to side to loosen up. She breathes out a happy sigh, jumps out of bed with a skip and goes to the bathroom. She splashes water on her face and grabs a face towel to pat it down. Pausing for a moment, she stares at the person in the mirror. The seemingly new person in the reflection instils a sense of satisfaction. Her attention shifts to her unkempt hair. She opens the top drawer of the vanity, searching for a hairbrush. The drawer only opens halfway, but she lunges her forearm all the way to the back to feel some spikey bristles. She drags the hairbrush out through the clutter and assesses it, since she hasn't used it in a while. Satisfied, she then brushes and fixes her hair into a neat style. She heads to the kitchen and turns on the kettle to make herself a cup of coffee. Sipping on her coffee, she looks around her lounge room. She's so used to living in darkness, it hasn't dawned on her today that it's actually quite dark inside. Suddenly, she's struck by an epiphany—she slowly puts the coffee down and beams through the thoughtful revelation. She hurries to the closet and grabs a couple of cardboard boxes. She places the boxes on the lounge room table and ties her hair back into a ponytail. She sets her gaze on the stale, out-of-date curtains like a woman on a mission. Those curtains have been frozen in time, not having felt the breeze in seven years. She marches toward the curtains that have held back the light for so long. She slides her hands between them, to where they meet in the middle. She takes a deep breath and, with all her might, thrusts the curtains open. The accumulation of seven years of fine dust is flung into the air. She basks in the warm sunlight that bursts through the window. She had forgotten how wonderful the warm sun felt on her skin. She closes her eyes and breathes in deeply. Suddenly, she forcefully coughs, overcome by the surrounding dust haze. She attempts to open the window, but it's stuck. She hammers the wooden frame with the side of her fist. The jolts loosen the frame, and she is able to open the window all the way, waving the dust away from her face. She puts her hands on her hips and turns her attention to the lounge room. She grabs the tangible memories, trinkets, and photo frames and packs them into the boxes—any reminders of the past. She feels a sense of relief with each item she packs away, mumbling to herself. *It's time to start a new life.*

It's 3:58 pm. The boxes are full. They sit on top of the lounge armchair she used for years as a bed, another one of the items she will be replacing.

It's delivery day and Stan pulls up in front of her house. He grabs her groceries from the back of the truck and walks to her front door.

"Huh … the curtains are open," he mutters with surprise. He knocks. Ms. Davis promptly opens the door. Stan takes a step back in disbelief. He's not accustomed to seeing her smile, or looking presentable!

"Hello Stan, how are you today?" She asks cheerfully. He fumbles his words.

"I … Uh … I'm going well, Ms. Davis." He's not quite sure what to make of this surprising greeting. He looks at the groceries and holds up the box. "I have your weekly delivery."

"Oh, thank you." She grabs the groceries from him, placing them on the table next to her. But she pulls out the bottle of Wittman's Whiskey and hands it back to him.

"Could you please refund this item on my tab and remove it from all future deliveries?"

"Sure … will do, Ms. Davis."

"Actually, cancel all future orders. I'm going to do my own shopping from now on."

"Oh … okay, Ms. Davis."

"Please, call me 'Helen'."

He nods his head. "Okay." He loosens up a little. "Helen, are you feeling alight? You seem … different, good different." She laughs, leans on the doorframe, and ponders for a moment,

"I'm doing great … I guess you could say I've finally seen the light."

∞

Bruce is rummaging through a garbage bin. He pulls out two empty soft drink bottles. He squeezes them into his makeshift trolley, which has now reached capacity. He grabs the trolley handle and heads to the recycling depot. He places his collection on the counter so the attendant can count the cans and bottles.

"Three dollars and twenty cents," says the attendant.

He holds out his hand, and the attendant gives him the cash. "Thank you."

Bruce hobbles to the nearby convenience store. He couples the recent payment with the payment from yesterday's haul and is able to buy a ham and cheese sandwich and a bottle of water. He sits on an empty milk crate out front of the convenience store, munching away contently on his sandwich. He's reminded of the time Manny gave him half a sandwich—a moment of kindness he'll always remember. He stares intently at his trolley, trying to figure out how to create more space to pack in more bottles and cans. Then, as he looks out into the distance, his attention shifts to a homeless person sleeping against a wall across the road. He finishes eating his sandwich and crosses the road. The person lies zipped within a grimy sleeping bag, covering their body from head to toe. The only movements are the gentle up-and-down puffs of slumber. He stands there for a moment, contemplating how he could help when, as he well knows, he doesn't exactly have the means. Noticing a torn cap nearby, he reaches into his pocket and pulls out all his remaining change. He looks at the change in his hands, then at the sleeping person. He places the change in the cap and continues down the street.

After a time, as he walks by the Gospel Mission Church, the sign out front catches his attention. It reads, "Community day today. All are welcome." The pastor is out front talking to people, welcoming them as they walk in. Bruce stares at the sign wondering if *he* would be welcome. The pastor sees Bruce looking at the sign and calls out to him.

"Hello … would you like to come in, sir?" Bruce looks at him but remains still. He ponders the invitation. *Would he really be welcome?* In his mind, surely he'll be rejected, just like he has been most of his homeless life. He wants to protect himself from another rejection. The pastor calls out again.

"You're most welcome to come join us if you like, there's no judgment here. Jesus doesn't turn anybody away." The mention of "Jesus" gets Bruce's attention. He remembers what Manny said about Jesus' love for him. He's not a religious man, nor did he know much about Jesus. His late wife had been a church-going, Bible-reading woman who prayed regularly. She had tried gently to get Bruce to accompany her to church, but he never did. In hindsight, he wishes he had gone with her, to have spent more time with her and to understand more about Jesus. Finally, his curiosity to find out more about this "Jesus" gets the better of him. He takes tentative steps up the church pathway. The pastor notices Bruce's hesitation and waits for him patiently. He sticks out his hand.

"I'm Pastor Robert."

Bruce looks down at his hand, in disbelief that someone wants to shake his hand. He looks up at Pastor Robert, smiles, and says in his husky, toughened tone, "Bruce." He proceeds to shake his hand.

"Great to meet you, Bruce … come on in." Pastor Robert places his hand on Bruce's shoulder and guides him inside.

∞

The children lounge around the television as the day winds down into evening. Amanda is finishing off the day's paperwork before her shift ends. While shuffling through some documents, she comes across Doctor Fletcher's business card. She picks it up and stares at it affectionately. She grabs her phone and heads out to the patio to be alone. She dials. The call reaches his message bank. *You've reached Doctor Fletcher. Please leave a message.* Beep. She's disappointed she can't talk to him but leaves a message anyway.

"Hi Thom … it's Amanda. I just wanted to thank you again for coming by this morning. It really helped me out a lot … anyway, hope we can catch up soon … bye."

∞

Doctor Fletcher puts on his white overcoat and grabs his clipboard to begin his evening shift. He heads out his office and down the hall to his first patient. On his way, the hospital fun board catches his eye. He stops, turns, and walks over to the fun board. A photograph arrests his attention. It's a photo of Manny and Amanda, taken by Dimples the Clown on the day they first met. He smiles as he admires the photograph. He slowly reaches up to grab it when a nurse interrupts him.

"Doctor Fletcher, you're needed in Room 26." He hurries off, leaving the photograph on the board.

∞

Max sits up in bed, in deep contemplation, gazing out the window. His thoughts are interrupted when the other boys shuffle in their sleep. He's prepared to drop back down in his bed if they wake up. He doesn't want anyone to see him up late at night. It might be silent around him but certainly not within. The disparaging voices in his mind have hampered his slumber for as long as he can remember. Now, though, a new voice has entered the arena. The voice of Manny's affirmation. All vying to gain supremacy on the battlefield of his mind. He struggles to reconcile the words spoken by Manny—that his life matters—with the abusive words of his parents, who'd belittled and degraded his life. He knows they can't both be right. But he doesn't know who to believe. He wants to believe Manny's words more than anything else but is haunted by the reality of his own life experience, and the fact that his own parents want nothing to do with him. To him, that fact all but confirms his worst fear … that no one loves him or wants him. Yet he can't shake off Manny's words. There seems to be a ring of truth about them, that he was born for a reason—he just wished he knew what that was. He grabs his book from the bedside table and opens it to the pages where he's written negatively about himself. He stares at the pages, becoming increasingly agitated.

In a sudden outburst of silent anger, he rips out all the pages, scrunching them up and throwing them across the room. Breathing heavily, he gets out of bed and walks toward the window. He looks upward into the night sky and whispers, "God, if what Manny said is true, show me how much you love me!"

For Such a Time as This

For we are God's handiwork, created in Christ Jesus to do good works, which God prepared in advance for us to do.

– Ephesians 2:10 (NIV)

Max sits in his corner of the patio, disengaged from the sounds of mid-morning enjoyment. He nibbles on his fingernails in deep thought. His attention is grabbed by an excited shrill; Abby is amused by a big, red bouncy ball she's playing with. Not immune to the natural laws of mimetic desire, Max wants what she has. He rushes toward her and snatches the ball away from her and starts bouncing it. Abby begins to cry. Manny, attentive to Abby's cries, approaches Max and politely intervenes.

"She was playing with the ball first, Max."

"Well, I'm playing with it now."

He accidentally bounces the ball on the tip of his shoe and it rolls toward Manny, who picks it up. Max lunges toward him.

"Give it back!" Max says, while grabbing the ball from Manny's hands, knocking him to the ground. Manny struggles to get up. He lies on the ground, clutching his chest, gasping for air. Rosie notices his distress.

"Miss Grace, Miss Grace!" She shouts urgently. Amanda pokes her head out from inside.

"What's going—" She stops mid-sentence when she sees Manny on the ground in distress. "Manny!"

She hurries to her desk to grab her phone, dials 911, then hurries to be with Manny, kneeling next to him.

"It's okay, Manny, we're going to get help." She shifts her conversation to the phone. "Yes, it's an emergency!"

∞

Pale and fatigued, Manny rests beneath a large beeping machine. Colorful lines on the screen skip irregularly, monitoring his heartbeat. Amanda looks deeply concerned. She stands by his bedside while Doctor Fletcher analyzes data and takes notes. He motions to Amanda to come over by the door.

"I'm afraid it's not looking good," he whispers. She lets out a deflated sigh. "The sudden knock to the ground placed an immense strain on his heart, severely damaging the muscles that pump the blood around the body. His condition is deteriorating by the hour. He's on borrowed time now. There's nothing more we can do." Deeply saddened, she turns her gaze to Manny.

His eyelids flutter. "Doc," he calls faintly. They rush to his side.

"Yes, Manny, I'm here."

"Am I going home soon?"

"I'm afraid not, little buddy. I don't think you'll be heading back to the orphanage any time soon."

"No … I mean … home to heaven." Suddenly grief-stricken, Amanda places her trembling hand over her mouth to suppress her emotions. Doctor Fletcher clenches his teeth and looks away for a moment to compose himself.

"Sorry, Manny … I wish there was more we could do for you," he says.

"Don't be sorry, Doc, we're all here for a time and a purpose. When that time will end, no one knows for sure. That's why you've got to make the most of every day, to live with purpose and hope … and to be that hope for others." Doctor Fletcher listens intently; a stray tear runs down his cheek. Amanda stands by his bedside, wiping away unceasing tears. Manny continues. "I hope I've made a difference."

Doctor Fletcher nods, clears his throat. "You have, Manny … you certainly have."

Amanda sits on the edge of his bed. "You've made a lasting difference in my life, Manny." She places her hand on his.

∞

The children are asleep earlier than usual. It had been an emotionally exhausting day. The children watched on in stunned silence as their much-loved friend Manny was tended to by paramedics and taken away by an ambulance. Sadness and tears filled the solemn atmosphere for the rest of the day. Max lies awake, consumed by the days' incident. He didn't mean to hurt Manny—it wreaks havoc on his mind to know that he caused him harm. The consideration he gave to Manny's positive affirmation regarding him—initially causing him to second-guess his parents' condemnations—is completely dashed. The faint hope of a purposeful, worthwhile life is gone. He settles again on believing the words of his parents: that his life is meaningless, and that he is a mistake. He sits up in bed and inspects the room. Content that the other boys are fast asleep, he quietly gets out of bed. He grabs his exercise book to write something. He tears out the page as quietly as possible and leaves it on the pillow. Max puts on his hoodie, slips on his shoes, and moves toward the window. One of the boys tosses and turns subtly. He crouches down so as not to be seen, remaining still until the movement stops. When the coast is clear, he carefully opens the window, which is known to squeak when opened quickly, and climbs out. He makes his way through the bushes beneath the window and runs across the front yard, past the orphanage gate to the street. In his haste, he runs across the street without looking. A car rounds the bend. Max freezes with shock in the headlights. A screech of breaks, then a thud.

∞

Max lays bruised and unconscious on a stretcher; he's rushed through the halls of the hospital, straight into emergency theater. Amanda has dosed off in a chair by Manny's bedside. Her cell phone rings. In a dazed stupor, she sits up slowly, assuming the buzz is coming from the medical equipment before realizing it's her phone.

"Hello," she answers, rubbing her face and sitting back in her chair. "Helen!" Amanda is surprised she has called at such a late hour. Shocked, she listens, sits up abruptly. "Oh my goodness!" She runs out the room to the reception desk.

"Excuse me, is there a young boy here, Max Harris?" The nurse checks the computer records.

"Yes … he was struck by a vehicle … and is currently in theater." She points down the hall.

"Thankyou."

She runs down the hall and sees Doctor Fletcher ahead, outside the theater room, about to enter. Panicked, she calls out to him.

"Thom!" She runs up to him. "Thom, is Max going to be okay?"

"We need to operate immediately. We'll have a better understanding after surgery." He disappears hastily into the theater room. Amanda is overwhelmed; she leans back against the wall to catch her breath, shaken by the day's events.

She stays in Manny's room in the following hours, wrestling with intermittent sleep. Each time she dozes off, thoughts of Max or Manny jolt her awake. Awake once again, she peers through heavy eyes and checks on Manny. He's still sleeping. She looks out the window and notices the first dim light of dawn; she looks down at her phone to check the time. Fatigued, she rubs her face, folds her arms, and walks out the room. She stops in the hallway and looks around. She spots Doctor Fletcher down the hall talking to another doctor. She strolls toward him and waits nearby. When their conversion ends, he turns to Amanda.

"Amanda … you look exhausted." Concerned, he places his hand on her upper arm.

"How's Max?"

"We managed to stabilize him but he's in a critical condition … he's lost a lot of blood, and we need to

replenish it soon. We're working urgently on that."
Amanda sighs in relief. "You need to look after yourself,
take a break, go home and refresh. I'm here all morning.
I'll call you immediately if there are any developments."

She nods in agreement. "Thank-you, Thom."

She walks back to Manny's room and grabs her purse.
She leans over him and whispers. "I'll be back soon."
He's unresponsive. She kisses him on the forehead and
walks out.

∞

Amanda feels refreshed after a brief stint at home,
but concerning thoughts of Max and Manny weigh
heavily on her mind. She enters the orphanage; the
children are on the patio having their breakfast. Ms.
Davis sees her walk in through the glass door and steps
inside.

"Morning, Helen."

"Morning, Amanda, how are things?"

"They could be better." She sighs. "Thank you for
covering my shift today."

"You're most welcome. How are the boys?"

"Max is in a stable condition, but Manny … it's not
good." Ms. Davis is visibly saddened by the news.

"I've been praying for them." Amanda is comforted by her compassion.

"I'm going to grab some of Max's things and head back to the hospital." Ms. Davis leans in and hugs Amanda.

"If you need anything, you just let me know."

"Thank you, I will. You've been such a great help already." They break the embrace and Amanda ponders for a moment.

"Helen … can I ask … what happened to you?" Ms. Davis giggles.

"Let's just say a little angel told me something I needed to hear." At first, Amanda wonders what she means. Then, she realizes who she must be referring to.

"Manny?"

Ms. Davis nods and smiles.

"Of course."

Amanda rummages through Max's closet; she grabs a bag and throws it on Max's bed. She picks out some of his clothes and puts them in the bag. While packing, she glances toward the pillow and notices the note. She stops packing and picks it up.

It's all my fault.
I'm a mistake.

I shouldn't have been born.
I'm leaving for good, it's best for everyone.

She sighs and murmurs, "Oh Max."

∞

Amanda places the bag of Max's clothes on the guest chair. She hovers over Max and places her hand on his arm, hoping to get a reaction, but he doesn't move. She looks up at the machines he's wired to, keeping him alive. She spends a few moments by Max's bedside then walks down the hall to check on Manny. He's awake, but struggling to keep his eyes open. She sits on the edge of the bed, leans in toward him and softly speaks.
"Hey Manny … How are you feeling today?"
"I'm okay."
"Manny, I need to tell you something." At this point, Doctor Fletcher enters the room. "Max was in an accident last night."
"What happened?" He asks, concerned. "Is he okay?" Doctor Fletcher interrupts.
"He's in a stable condition. But he's lost a lot of blood and needs a transfusion as soon as possible. Unfortunately, his blood type is hard to find and is quite

119

rare. AB negative. The recent train derailment in Buford County reduced supplies of all the blood banks in the area. We're doing all we can to source a supply."

Manny looks at Amanda. "That's my blood type, isn't it?"

"Yeah, it is."

Manny turns to Doctor Fletcher. "He can have my blood."

Doctor Fletcher and Amanda briefly share a look.

"You still need your blood, Manny," Doctor Fletcher says.

"It's okay. Not much longer now, I won't need it anymore."

Amanda strokes his arm, deeply moved by his self-sacrificing offer.

"We're checking with all the donor centers and hospitals in the neighboring cities. Hopefully, we'll find a supply shortly."

"Thank-you, Doctor." Amanda says. He nods and walks out the room.

"Manny, there's something else about Max. As I was packing some of his things, I found this note." She hands it to him. "I thought you'd want to know."

He holds up the letter; it shakes in his frail hand as he reads it. Manny puts it down and considers what he has just read. He turns to Amanda. "Can you grab a pen and notepad?"

∞

The rhythmic beeps, faint distant footsteps of the medical staff, and the general hum of the late night hospital atmosphere have lulled Amanda to sleep. Manny calls out faintly.

"Miss Grace … Miss Grace."

She is awakened by the irregular sound and hastens to his bedside. "I'm here, Manny." She places her hand on his shoulder.

"I'm going now."

It takes a moment before she realizes what he means. She runs out of the room, searching for Doctor Fletcher; he's at the reception desk talking to a nurse. She calls out and motions for him to come quickly. He hurries to Manny's room. Amanda runs back to Manny's side. She leans in close and grabs his hand. Doctor Fletcher comes to his bedside, opposite Amanda.

"Tell everyone at the orphanage I'll miss them." Amanda's face crumples with grief; her chin begins to tremble. "And tell Abby, she'll have a real mommy and daddy soon."

"You deserved the love of a real parent, Manny," she says. "I'm sorry you didn't get that chance."

Manny raises his hand from her grasp to cup her cheek.

"I did have that love … Mommy." Profoundly moved by his declaration, she squeezes her eyelids shut as streams race down her cheeks; she exhales a sigh through quaking lips. She cups her hand over his and leans into his hand. She smiles through the tears, thankful for the special moment of connection with him, and the sense of redemption it provides her. "Thank you so much, Manny." She takes hold of his hand, gently moves it toward her mouth, and kisses it.

"I'm going to miss you, Manny," Doctor Fletcher says. He strains to keep his emotions from showing. "You're a special little guy. It's not fair you have to go through this."

Manny gathers his last breaths.

"If it wasn't for such a time as this, you wouldn't have met Miss Grace." Doctor Fletcher and Amanda briefly glance at each other—they know he's right. "Certain people cross paths because they need each other. Sometimes they don't even know it." With his last ounce of strength, Manny reaches out his frail arm toward Doctor Fletcher, who gives his hand to Manny. Manny then takes hold of Amanda's hand, which she's still holding close to her mouth. He brings their hands together over his chest till they are touching fingertip-to-fingertip, hand-to-hand. By their own will, they cross fingers to clasp hands. Manny's hands lose grip and fall away from their hands, lifeless.

The Gift

But those who hope in the Lord will renew their strength. They will soar on wings like eagles; they will run and not grow weary, they will walk and not be faint.

– Isaiah 40:31 (NIV)

The events of recent weeks weigh on Max's mind as he packs his belongings in his bag pensively. Doctor Fletcher and Amanda stroll into the room as he explains Max's course of medication and an upcoming hospital appointment.

"How are you feeling, Max? It's been a tough couple of weeks, but you pulled through quite well." Doctor Fletcher says.

He shrugs his shoulders. "I'm okay," he says, continuing to pack.

Doctor Fletcher turns to Amanda. "I'll leave you to it. Any problems, just let me know."

"Thank you, Doctor."

"I've got your discharge papers. You good to go, Max?" Amanda says. Despondently, Max nods and turns to face her.

"Miss Grace … why did Manny give me his blood when it was all my fault?" Suddenly, Amanda remembers the letter Manny wrote the night he heard about Max's accident. He had asked her to give the letter to Max when he recovered. She searches through her bag.

"Here." She hands him an envelope. "Manny wanted me to give you this when you recovered." He takes the letter with trepidation. "Read it, take your time. I'll meet you outside when you're done." She leaves Max alone with the letter.

He stares at his name written on the front of the envelope, written by Manny's unsteady hand. He hesitates to open it. He expects Manny's last words to him to contain anger, blame, and condemnation—which is what he thinks he deserves after what he did to him. However, he believes he at least owes it to Manny to give him the right to make a final declarative verdict about the value of his life. He opens the envelope, sighs in resignation, ready to accept the contents, pulls out the letter and unfolds it.

Max,

I hope you get this letter. That means you made it through ok. I want to let you know I don't hate you. What happened to me is not your fault. I was already sick. It was just my time to go. We're all put on earth for a purpose, and if my only purpose was to help you live, then I'm glad I was here for that purpose. We all go through tough times in life, most of the time we didn't do anything to deserve it. The past can keep you down, if you let it. You can allow what you've been through to hurt others, or you can allow what you've been through to help others. What will you do Max? Why not replace the lies with the truth—and here is the truth. You are not a mistake. You are alive for a reason and God has an amazing plan for your life. It's your choice Max. The path you take is up to you. Always remember, no matter what you've been through, no matter what you've done, you are known and loved by God.

Your friend,
Manny

His mouth progressively slackens as he reads through the letter. Years of accumulated anguish seep from the corner of his eyes, pooling, gradually blurring his vision. He breathes deeper; he's confused about what he's reading, yet he feels the relief wash over his afflicted heart. As he finishes reading, his eyes can no longer contain the deluge. A downpour of tormented drops falls onto the page. He feels as though he's signing the bottom of the letter with his tears, in agreement to Manny's declarations about his life—finally liberating a captive and tortured soul.

Doctor Thomas Fletcher and Amanda Grace

Doctor Fletcher squints as he reads his screen, the glare beginning to irritate his eyes in the growing darkness. He turns on the desk lamp. The light reflects from a frame containing a photo of Sophie and Ruby. He leans back in his chair and reminisces about the day it was taken. He opens the top desk drawer and pulls out the bottle of pills, holds it in front of him and ponders for a moment. Hastily, he jumps out of his chair and runs to the adjoining bathroom. He turns the tap on full blast and pours the contents of the pill bottle down the drain. He throws the bottle into the trash and turns off the tap. Hands out in front of him, he leans on the counter, hangs his head and closes his eyes. He takes in a deep breath and holds it, before lifting his head and opening his eyes to look into the mirror; he gazes at the man staring back at him. He knows that the person he's become is not the person his wife and daughter would want him to be. In this final confrontation with the man in the mirror, Doctor Fletcher stares him down before letting out a strained mutter. *Goodbye.* He breathes out with an emancipatory sigh, leaving behind that miserable man in the reflective glass. He walks back to his desk and picks up a handwritten note. It's from Amanda, and it reads, *Anytime you need to talk*, with her number below.

Amanda sits contentedly, looking up at the twilight sky while she sips on her chamomile tea. She turns her gaze to the blue poppy in the middle of the garden and admires the recent bloom that signals the start of a new season. This season's bloom holds more significance than usual—the blue flowers and freckles of yellow have never been more vibrant. To Amanda, it feels like the new birth of her own life. The sign in the ground that had space for a name is now engraved with "Manny." She closes her eyes and takes a deep breath. A piece of her fringe, that had been tucked behind her ear, drops out of place onto her cheek. A light breeze caresses her face and gently shifts the hanging fringe. It's the same side of her face on which Manny placed his hand that night at the hospital; the subtle breezy caress reminds her of him. She smiles at the thought and takes another sip of her tea. Her phone rings. She picks it up from the bench.

"Hello." She smiles at the sound of the voice on the end of the line. "Hey Thom …"

Life doesn't always go the way you want it to. You could be living the perfect life one moment, but in the next, it can all come crashing down. You're stuck in an uncontrollable circumstance that has you questioning everything you believe. Or your life plan is destroyed by a poor choice that haunts you. It feels like you've lost everything, and you're barely holding onto any strands of faith or hope. And if they're gone, what else is there? However, keep holding onto those remnants of faith and hope; this is all you need to keep going. God can use the broken pieces in your life and join them with someone else's broken pieces to make sense. It's through the brokenness that the light can shine the most. You may not understand this because you don't see the bigger picture, but God does. Fear and concern about what the future holds can

Helen Davis

Helen laughs boisterously, without restraint, unconcerned by the glares of other patrons. She collects her breath, then wipes away her joyful tears. She radiates happiness through her gasps. "Oh my goodness. This is the most I've laughed in years."

Stan nods with satisfaction. "I'm glad my delivery mishaps bring someone a little joy."

She leans back in her chair as her lighthearted demeanor becomes more serious. "Thank you so much for tonight. To be honest, I'm surprised you asked me out … especially after the way I treated you at first."

"Nah, I could tell there was a special lady underneath that hardened veneer." He smirks.

She appreciates his kind words with a tilt of her head. "But you didn't have to bring me here to L'Amour. It's pricey!"

"I know, but you've had a rough time the past few years and you deserve to be treated well after everything you've been through."

Bashfully, she shakes her head.

"You know … I wish I hadn't waited so long to live life again. This is the first time in a long time I've felt … free."

Emmanuel

The hurt that someone else has caused you can leave a deep scar. The aching heart is desperate for closure, and you're convinced that you can't have any hope until you get the answers you want. But hope deferred makes the heart sick. The more time that passes without the answers, the harder your heart becomes. And the longer you withhold forgiveness, the stronger it becomes in controlling you. The wound sinks ever deeper to the point of numbing the desire to properly live, and love again, sending you into a dark place. You build walls to protect yourself and shut everyone out, making it hard for you to trust anyone. But to live without love is to exist without living. When you don't forgive, it harms you more than anybody else. And forgiveness doesn't mean forgetting; it means releasing the person who hurt you from weighing you down. It's a decision, not a feeling. If you wait until you feel like forgiving, you can become trapped in a prison of resentment.

No matter what anyone has done to you, no matter how they may have treated you, you are loved and treasured by God. And nothing in all creation can break his love for you.

Bruce Douglas

Bruce dusts the lint from the collar of his dark blue pin-striped suit. He's quite pleased with his recent thrift store purchase, complete with matching fedora; it reminds him of his favorite suit from his late teens, when he first courted his wife. He hobbles out of his bedroom and stops by the kitchen counter. He pulls thirty dollars from his front jacket pocket and slips it in the share house rent collection box. Exiting the house, he heads down the street, whistling a happy tune. There's a joy in his hobbling step and an infectious warmth about him. Passersby notice his delightful manner—so much so, he's become known within the community as "delightful Doug." He acknowledges everyone that passes him by: a nod of the hat, a wave, and a "how do you do" are his standard greetings. He enters the local homeless shelter and places his suit jacket and fedora on the coat rack, then weaves through the hall packed with people eating their breakfast meals. He greets and is greeted by everyone who crosses his path. He enters the kitchen, puts on an apron, and takes his place at the counter to serve the meals.

Emmanuel

It's been said that loneliness is the greatest sickness in the world. When you lose everything you've ever known and loved, life can feel empty and the world can be an unforgiving place. There's no aching of the heart like the feeling of being rejected and treated like you're worthless. You can do the greatest things for others and still be unappreciated. The heart becomes cynical and the question, "what's the point of living?" becomes a valid option to the person lurking in the darkness. But your worth and value aren't related to the worlds' value system; your worth and value are determined by what God gave up for you.

When all others have abandoned you, it might feel like God has abandoned you too! Remember this—you may not always see his hand at work in your life, but you can always trust in his heart.

Max Harris

Abby is on the play mat, constructing a house with building blocks. Max enters the room and walks up to her. He stops and stands beside her, at first unbeknownst to Abby, then sits down next to her, grabs a building block and hands it to her. Trevor, who arrived at the orphanage last night, enters the play area. Max is intrigued by his interactions with the other children. Trevor disrupts the other children as they're playing; he throws toys around and picks on a few others. Max recognizes something familiar in this; he's exhibiting the same behaviors and characteristics that Max displayed when he was his age. Trevor approaches Abby and Max, and Max gets up from the floor. Trevor looks down at Abby building her blockhouse. With a grimace, he swings his leg back to knock it down. Max quickly interjects, sticking out his hand. "Wait!" Trevor looks up at him with his leg still cocked ready to swing forward.

"My parents don't want me either," Max says.

Trevor's whole countenance changes. He becomes passive, dropping his leg back down to stand still. Max puts his hand on his shoulder. "It's okay. I'm going to help you through this." Trevor nods softly as tears run along his bottom eyelids.

Emmanuel

A cruel past might be all that you know. The echo of hurtful words can't be easily turned off. The harassing memories deceive the heart and mind, so that you begin to believe they are the truth. You may not be able to forget the abusive things that have been said or done to you. But you can overpower them and replace them—and even use them for good. Don't be confused by the ill treatment this world can sometimes inflict. There's only one truth: that you are God's child, and he gave everything he loved for you. That's the most important truth you need to know. There will be voices in this world that will try to drown out that truth. Don't let them. Hold to that truth more than anything else and turn the painful shadows of the past into today's hope. You can use what you've been through to help those who are struggling with the same troubles you've experienced—to be that gift to another.

Six months later

Amanda and Doctor Fletcher stand in front of Manny's headstone.

A little voice speaks. "Look Manny, I have a mommy and daddy now," says Abby. Amanda and Doctor Fletcher look at each other adoringly.

"Manny, you changed our lives. You were … you *are* truly a gift to us. You gave us the hope we needed. Amanda is now my wife and Abby our precious daughter."

"I'll never forget you, Manny. I miss you," says Amanda.

"Miss you too, Manny," Abby repeats.

They spend a few moments in silent contemplation.

Emmanuel

You rarely end up where you want to; but, almost always, you end up where you need to be. Moments may come that will change your life completely. But life is more than one moment; it's filled with many moments that help make you who you are. You don't want or ask for these moments; most of the time these moments seem to choose you. You don't know when you will meet a mountain or a valley; you might be facing one right now. There will be pain, there will be heartbreak, dreams may not be fulfilled, and others will hurt you. No one is immune to the pain and trouble of life, not even Jesus. When your time comes, you can stay stuck in that moment or you can move forward as best you can. The Shepherd's Psalm says, "even though I walk through the darkest valley ..." We walk through these dark moments, but we shouldn't stay there. When you remain still, you can miss the gift waiting for you on the journey. But the gift will not be withdrawn because of your circumstances. No matter how long you've dwelled there, as long as you're breathing, the gift remains on offer, always waiting for you. And remember—as long as there is God, there is hope.

The gift has been offered; the choice is yours to receive it or reject it. Your path in life and your destiny all come down to your willingness to respond to the gift. This amazing gift is free for anyone who will receive it; nothing needs to be given accept an open heart. This gift gives life anew, life abundantly filled with joyous hope, and that ... is the greatest gift of all.

Slowly, the three of them walk back to the car.

"You know … I don't think you ever told me what that note said, containing the scripture, you know… the one they found on Manny in the manger."

"Oh!" Amanda says, surprised. She ponders for a moment.

"It said … If the Son sets you free, you will be free indeed … Thanks be to God for his indescribable gift!"

If the Son sets you free, you will be free indeed

- John 8:36 (NIV)

Thanks be to God for his indescribable gift!

- 2 Corinthians 9:15 (NIV)

Other books by Peter Tonna

Non-Fiction

OUR FATHER

Who is God? What is He like? Is He distant? Does He care? In this brief, yet informational book, I shed light on the character of God; how He relates to us; and touch on some of the most searching questions about God. Yes, God is mysterious but when you look into the scriptures, the Bible, you see just how much God has revealed Himself to humanity, especially through Jesus. There is more than enough scriptural evidence to show who God is, His character, and His concern and love for all of humanity. God is not a distant deity that has zero interest in his creation. Quite the opposite, He very much wants to be involved in every aspect of our lives to the smallest detail. This book is heavily backed by scripture, incorporating logical reason and existential evidence. There are an endless number of words and phrases to describe God, the one He wants us to refer to Him the most, as shown by Jesus, is father.

WORLD'S GREATEST INFLUENCER

Many, including those who profess the Christian faith, don't have a thorough understanding of what Jesus taught on certain issues. Many seem to think that Christianity supports racism, condones slavery and the oppression of women. I wrote this book to shed light on the truth about what Jesus taught and delve into the issues that affect our society today as much as it did 2,000 years ago. This book focuses on the influence and legacy of Jesus' life and teachings, particularly on topics such as; Women, Slavery, Racism, Politics, Ethics & Morality, Love and Religion. I delve into the not-so-obvious truths that might otherwise be overlooked. I also explain the meaning and context of some of the questionable passages that seem to contradict Jesus' teachings. While Jesus is both divine and human, I focus on Jesus–the man–his human side, appealing to people of all faiths and none.

www.poete.com.au/books

https://books2read.com/TheUnwantedGift

https://books2read.com/WorldsGreatestInfluencer

https://books2read.com/OurFather

All books by Peter Tonna available most book outlets
around the world

9 780645 026474